# Three
# Courageous Women

# Three Courageous Women

Everyone is like a butterfly, they start out ugly and awkward and then morph into beautiful and graceful butterflies that everyone loves.

...Drew Barrymore

*(American actress, model, producer, director and author)*

Ray Weaver

Sirena Press
Madeira Beach, Fl

Three Courageous Women
Copyright © 2015 Ray Weaver

ISBN 978-0-9856851-6-4

Other books by Ray Weaver: available on Amazon.com
Tightrope to Justice
Miami Justice
European Justice
Justice 4 Willis
Final Justice

For information:
raymondellie@aol.com

Cover and Book Design
The Murmaid tm
for Sirena Press

Printed in the United States of America

First American Edition

# Dedication

This novel is dedicated to the three wonderful ladies

who have been in my life.

My mother, Marie, who made sure I received a good education

and helped to shape my character as a man.

My wife, Ellie, who encouraged, helped, and pushed

me to write my six novels.

Next, to my daughter, Denise, of whom

I'm extremely proud.

Lastly, a tribute to all the courageous women of history,

who fought to have their voices heard.

A special thanks to all who have purchased these stories

and to those who have so kindly offered positive

feedback and constructive critiques.

And finally, a special thanks to my editor and publisher,

Nancy Frederich for her enhancement of the stories

and the exciting covers.

# Contents

# Married To The Army

## Chapter 1

"Bernadine, your friend April is here," Zeva Hurley called out to her granddaughter, who was in the back bedroom of their small two story brick home. In her late sixties, Zeva was short, with a stocky build and gray hair drawn back into a severe bun.

Zeva had spent her whole life living in the small town of Middleton, New York, a small community not far from the West Point Academy. She had retired after twenty five years at Macys Department Store. When her son and his wife were killed in an automobile accident, their two year old daughter, Bernadine, had come to live with the widowed Zeva in her modest home. Zeva had spent the last two decades caring for her granddaughter; not only making sure that she had a good education, but filling her life with love and devotion.

After Bernadine started her job at the bank, she said to her grandmother, "Once I start making big money Nana, I'm going to get us a better place and all new furniture. That's the least I can do in return for all that you have done for me."

"I'll be down in five minutes, Nana," Bernadine yelled down from her upstairs room. The twenty-two year old was tall and slender with hair the color of raven's wings. Long and wavy, it cascaded down her back like a waterfall. Even more striking were her eyes which were like sapphires set in her lovely face with its natural rose blush.

Bernadine checked her appearance in the faded mirror above the old bedroom dresser. She carried herself gracefully, almost like a queen.

"Where are you two off to April?" Zeva asked her granddaughter's friend as the two waited for Bernie's appearance.

April was a spectacular-looking petite girl with short white-blond hair that curled around her lightly freckled face. April smiled and replied, "The boys at West Point Military Academy have Easter week off. The guys who didn't go home for the holidays rented the back room at Wesley's Bar and Grill Restaurant for a private party. My boyfriend, Max, invited Bernie and me to join them for a couple of drinks and some burgers. And, Max has someone special that he wants her to meet."

Loving spring and glad to shed her heavy winter coat, Bernadine entered the living room with a black suede jacket casually draped across her arm.

"That sounds like it might be a pleasant time." Zeva looked with pride at her granddaughter. She was neatly dressed in the high of the nineties fashion, a short black skirt, a white crop top sweater and black wedgie shoes.

"You look very nice dear," Zeva said. "But, let's give those other girls some competition."

She proceeded to adjust the top of Bernie's cardigan. "Now, that's more like it. You and April, go wow those young cadets. I'm an expert in fashion you know," she added, turning to April. "I worked for Macy's high-end dress department for years."

Zeva knew April was a well mannered Catholic girl and she had no fear of her granddaughter associating with her. In fact, April had been dating Maxfield Turner, a West Point Cadet, for some time and had even brought him to Zeva's home for Thanksgiving dinner.

Bernie grinned at her Nana. "You won't be upset if I bring home a soldier will you?"

Zeva laughed in return. "No Dear. Just have a good time. And keep a look out for a nice tall one like Grandpa Harry."

"Will do and don't wait up for me," Bernie answered.

"Let's move," April said taking Bernie by the arm and propelling her out the front door.

As the girls walked down the sidewalk to the car, they could see Grandma Zeva peeking out of the front window. What they did not see, was Zeva, as she put her hands together and prayed, "Please God, help my Bernie find a nice young man and give her a future filled with happiness."

"Where is this Wesley's Bar and Grill?" Bernie asked as she jumped into the passenger seat of April's car.

"Just outside of town. About five miles from here. Should only take about fifteen minutes to get there." April switched on the car's ignition and pulled away from the curb. "Max is going to meet us there."

"You two seem to have been getting very serious lately."

A muscle jerked in April's cheek. She did not respond verbally.

Then, with a broad smile, Bernie looked over at her and asked, "Do you think that you can find a nice cadet for me tonight?"

April glanced at her. "Well. Well. My quiet friend is turning into a blossoming flower."

"I have to admit that I haven't been getting out much lately." Bernie expelled her breath in a long sigh.

April nodded. "It does seem like you've been working some long hours at that damn bank."

"In a small town like Middleton, the bank manager wants all the business that he can get so he keeps on pushing everyone. " Bernie cleared her throat. 'He calls it cross-selling'. And, who knows, there's talk that he's planning on moving and his job may be available. I want to be in a position to apply for it, if that happens."

With a dismissal wave of her hand, April changed the subject. "Enough business talk. Let me tell you about Max's new room-mate. He's supposed to be there tonight and we want you to meet him."

Bernie looked at her with amusement. "Always trying to fix me up, aren't you? Okay, give me the skinny on him."

"His name is Grant Alvin Younger III. And like Max, he's graduating from West Point this spring. And, I must say, my dear Bernie that he's very attractive."

Bernie laughed, a sheen of nervous sweat broke out on her lip.

"And when have I heard you say that before?"

"This time, I really mean it. He's just about as yummy as my Max," April said, as she pulled into the parking lot of the restaurant.

"And speaking of your boyfriend, Max. If the two of you want to leave the club early, don't let me spoil your night. You can always drop me off first or I'll find another way home," Bernie said with a self-conscious laugh.

"We'll see." April parked the car and they exited.

The owner of Wesley's Bar was an ex-Army sergeant and it was the local hang out. On week-ends it was taken over by the West Point cadets. A ten foot long wooden bar with two bartenders working full time dominated the one side of the room. Pictures on the wall were mostly scenes of old and new army battles. In the back of the bar were two private party rooms.

Entering the bar, they could smell beer and barbecued chicken wings. "Hope they have more than wings to eat," Bernie whispered to April. "I skipped supper."

They both looked up as a voice called out loudly. "April, over here."

"It's Max. Follow me," April pushed her way toward a table where several cadets, with beers in hand, were sitting.

"I'm right behind you," Bernie said, the muscles in the back of her neck tightening.

As April walked up to him, Max stood up. He had fine red hair and a receding hairline. And at six feet two he had to bend down to kiss April on the cheek. "Hi Doll. You're mine for the night."

Bernie grinned, thinking that this sounded like a well-rehearsed line.

"Come with me," Max said, leading them through the bar.

"My God, it's noisy in here," Bernie yelled out.

"It always is on Saturday nights," Max replied.

As they passed several of the young cadets, April introduced Bernie to them. Finally, Max led the girls to a table at the back of the room where a striking looking young cadet was seated.

"This is my room-mate, Grant Younger. Grant, you know, my

gal, April. And this is her friend, Bernadine."

As the young cadet stood up and reached out to shake her hand, Bernie could see that April had not been exaggerating. Grant was yummy—in fact, she thought he was drop-dead gorgeous. And Grandma would be pleased that he was so tall.

He appeared to be about six foot four and had sandy brown hair and a well-toned magnificent physique. Bernie immediately noticed his deep brown eyes that seemed to twinkle as he looked down at her. "I'm delighted to meet you, Bernadine. Please sit here beside me so that I can get to know you."

Bernie felt her cheeks flame. She inclined her head in graceful acknowledgement. She was so taken with this handsome young man, that she was almost tongue tied as she slid into the chair beside him.

A lightening grin crossed his face as Max leaned over and whispered, "Watch this guy, Bernie. He'll charm your head off."

"I thought you fellows rented a back room for your little party," April said to Max as she sat down beside him.

"Oh, we did. But it's crowded and noisy too, so we decided to sit here," Max replied.

As Grant slid his chair closer to Bernie, she looked up at him and asked shyly, "And what shall I call you Cadet Younger?"

"Grant is fine and you're Bernadine."

"Yes. But, I like to be called Bernie. Just plain Bernie," she said smiling up at him.

He took her hand in his. "Well, you're certainly not plain Bernie. In fact, where has April been hiding you?"

"Nowhere special," she answered. She smiled to herself, anxiousness and excitement coiling in the pit of her stomach. She controlled both with fierce determination. Cadet Younger was so charismatic and handsome.

"Boy, the noise in here is really terrible," April shouted out.

"Oh, you'll get used to it," Max replied. "Now, folks, what's your liking? I thought maybe a pitcher of beer and a tub of wings."

Grant looked at him and shook his head. "Why don't you order that for you and your girl? Actually, I'm starving and April is right—

it's awfully loud in here. Too loud to really get to know my new friend, Bernie."

Grant suddenly stood up. "Bernie, there's a nice restaurant just around the corner. Would you like to join me for a late supper and a nice quiet talk?"

Bernie thought for a few moments. "Do you think they may have vegetarian dishes?"

"I'm sure that they do. And as a matter of fact, I'm a vegetarian too. Let's go."

Bernie looked at April, her face reflecting the fact that she really wanted to get to know Grant better and asked, "Is that okay with you?"

"Sure," April replied. Then turning to Max, she added, "Beer and wings are fine with me, Max. Let's stay."

Max grinned at Grant. "You two go on. If you decide to come back, we'll be here for a while. Otherwise, just take your car and I'll have April take me back to the academy."

Grant took Bernie by the hand and led her out of the bar. "It's so nice out; let's walk to the restaurant, Bernadine."

"Please Grant, call me Bernie. I'm much more comfortable with that."

"Bernadine sounds very romantic and lovely, like you. But, if you prefer it, I will call you Bernie." He squeezed her hand. "Say, doesn't that air feel and smell fresh and clean," he said, drawing in a deep breath as they walked down the street to the corner restaurant.

Bernie looked at him. Suddenly, she wanted to know everything about him.

Entering "Ma's Restaurant," she noticed that it was half empty. Grant led her to a booth and helped her to slide in. Then, he took a seat on the wooden bench next to her. "Now, young lady, I'm in charge," he said with great confidence in his voice.

When the waitress approached, he said, "Miss, two of Mama's vegetarian dinner specialties, two iced teas and two house salads with blue cheese dressing." Then he looked briefly at Bernie, "Blue cheese okay?"

Stunned at the way that Grant seemed to take charge of the situation, she nodded her head in agreement. Her lips struggled to form the words. "Yes. That sounds good."

While they waited for the salads to arrive, Grant leaned back on the bench and grinned, "Okay, time for a few statistics. I need to know all about you."

Bernie smiled shyly, feeling for her composure and finally finding it. "Well, I'm twenty-two, single, work at a bank and live with my widowed grandmother. I lost my parents when I was very young. And what about you, Cadet Younger?"

"I'm twenty-three, single and will graduate from the academy later this year. My mother died a couple of years ago of a heart attack. My father is retired army, Colonel Grant Alvin Younger II, and lives in a retirement community. My grandfather, Grant Alvin Younger I, was a general in the army. Both of them are West Point graduates, so you see West Point and the army are not only our tradition, but, our way of life."

Bernie's solemn gaze met his as she tried to comprehend how this young cadet's future seemed to have been planned out for him already.

The waitress approached the table and set their salads and iced tea in front of them. Grant smiled charmingly at her. "Miss, don't hurry with the dinners," he ordered. "This young lady and I have all evening and lots to talk about."

Bernie chuckled as the waitress walked quickly away. "You are very military, Cadet Younger. But, then again, it sounds like it runs in the family." She could see also that he was very much at ease with the ladies and turning on the charm appeared to come easily to him.

He merely looked down at her and grinned, as she tried to gently change the subject. "I like this place, Grant. It's very quiet and has a nice atmosphere. Lots better than the bar."

"All the better to see you my Dear." He looked straight into her eyes. "I'm sure that, with your looks, you have many boyfriends and have heard all kinds of lines."

She shrugged her shoulders, slightly embarrassed, as she replied,

"Thanks for the compliment, but the truth is that I have none. Boyfriends, that is. I've been so busy working at the bank, since I graduated from college, that I haven't had much time to date. I decided not to waste my four years at Syracuse University to only become a teller. My aim is to be the first female manager of the Middletown Bank."

After the waitress brought their dinners, they ate quietly, talking about their likes and dislikes and their past lives. When they finished eating, Grant ordered refills on their teas and they continued to talk comfortably. They didn't notice the time and before they realized it a couple of hours had passed since they entered the restaurant.

Bernie looked over at Grant and stood up. "I need to use the ladies room. I'll be right back."

While she was gone, a heavy set older man approached the table and looked down at Grant and said in broken English, "Sir, I the owner of the place. I like to ask favor of you. As you can see, the place is now empty except for you two and if you are finished, I like to close. The weatherman said we get a hard storm and I have an hour drive home."

Grant looked up at him with a quick angry look and said indignantly, "The sign on your door says you're open until eleven. It's only ten-thirty." His features were grim and set, his jaw clenched.

The restaurant owner sighed, "I tell you," he added. "I take twenty percent off your bill if you'll leave now."

Grant let out a disgusted huff of air. "Give me the bill, we've leaving," he snapped.

"Thank you sir," the older man replied graciously, handing him the bill.

When Bernie came back from the ladies room, Grant gestured toward the man and said, "He wants us to leave now." His features were grim and set, his jaw clenched as he dropped money upon the table.

Bernie replied quietly. "I'm ready, Grant. The bench seemed to be getting hard anyway."

Grant jumped up, grabbed her by the hand and helped her off

the bench. Smiling reluctantly, he said, "You're right—let's go."

Bernie became aware of the fact that Grant made decisions rather quickly and could be a bit abrupt with people. At this point, she wasn't sure if she liked his behavior toward the restaurant owner, but she reasoned that perhaps his military training had taught him to always take charge.

As they walked down the street toward the car, a large bolt of lightning lit up the sky.

"Hey, the old guy was right. It looks like it's going to rain," Grant said begrudgingly.

"Should we go back inside the bar and see if April and Max are still there?" Bernie asked.

"No. I'm certain they're gone by now." Grant opened the car door and helped her inside. "I'll need directions on how to get to your house."

Later, as he pulled up beside her grandmother's house, Bernie looked over at Grant. "I would ask you inside but I think that my Nana will be asleep and I don't want to wake her."

"That's okay. I should get back to school and with the rain, it'll take me a while. I'll walk you to your door. But first, may I have your phone number?"

Bernie reached into her purse, pulled out her business card from the bank and wrote on it. Handing it to him, she breathed sharply before she spoke. "I put my home number on the back. If you call me at home, please don't make it too late, because my Nana goes to bed early."

He took the card from her and put it in his pocket. "Thanks."

He stepped out of the car, pulled an umbrella out from the floor of the back, opened it and walked around to the passenger side. He opened the door and gently helped Bernie exit as he held the umbrella over her.

Each got slightly wet as they walked together to the front. Bernie held out her hand to Grant. "Thanks for a delicious supper and a nice evening."

Grant placed the umbrella down on the porch, and, leaned closer to her, his eyes looking gently into hers. "If you don't mind, I'm going to kiss you."

Bernie lowered her hand. Her heart hammered wildly as he pulled her to his chest and gave her a passionate kiss on the lips.

Grant stepped back and smiled down on her. "If you're not busy Saturday, I'd like you to accompany me when I go to visit my father at the retirement home."

Her knees almost buckled. She looked at him with amazement. For the moment, Grant's softer side had emerged and even though he seemed to be moving quickly she thought that he was a very special guy. Yes, she was more attracted to him than she had ever been to any man.

She told herself to calm down, to ignore the rapid beating of her heart. "Yes. I think I'd like that. But, please call me Wednesday at the bank to confirm. I'm sure that I'll be able to go. My only problem is that if the bank auditors come in this week, I might have to work on Saturday."

He seemed elated that she had agreed to go with him. "I'll call you Wednesday at eleven hundred hours."

She stared at him with a puzzled look on her face.

"Oh yeah, that's military time. To you, that's eleven in the morning."

She nodded. "Yes. Okay."

"Looks like it's starting to rain harder. I better get going." Grant leaned over and gave her a second kiss—even longer and more passionate than the first one.

"I'll look forward to your phone call and going with you Saturday." Bernie couldn't breathe. She couldn't think. She had to force the words past lips that were almost numb.

"Great. And Bernie. Could you please pack a small lunch for the both of us?" He opened the door and she stepped inside. After she shut the door, he spun around; practically leaped off the porch and sprinted down the sidewalk to his car.

Bernie peered through the window and watched him drive off. Turning around, she noticed that there was a small light on in the kitchen. She felt like she was floating on air, as she walked down the dimly lighted hallway to the kitchen. She found her grandmother sitting calmly at the kitchen table.

"Oh Nana, what are you doing up?" Bernie asked as she rushed over to her, threw her arms around her shoulders and gave her a quick kiss on the top of her head.

"Been waiting up for you dear. I'll make you some hot chocolate. By the smile on your face, I believe that you might have had a very enjoyable evening."

"It was just wonderful," Bernie exclaimed as she slid onto the chair beside her grandmother. She was still shell-shocked. Her heart was racing.

"I have to admit that I was peeking out of the front window and noticed that young fellow who brought you home. So tell me all about this boy. I can't wait to hear the details."

Bernie looked at her grandmother solemnly. "Well, first of all, Nana. He's not a boy. He's a man and his name is Grant Alvin Younger, III and he's over six foot tall with a full head of sandy brown hair. He's a senior at West Point and graduates in the spring. His father and grandfather are also West Point graduates."

"Sounds like his whole family is very well educated," Zeva responded, somewhat amused at how Bernie was gushing on about her new acquaintance.

"Yes. Grant is extremely bright, a take charge kind of guy—very positive about everything. And, we seem to have a lot in common."

"Well, I saw him kiss you and you looked like you enjoyed it. You seem to have that in common," Zeva added.

"You were peeking out the window, Nana?"

"Well, only for a few minutes. Then, I headed back to the kitchen to wait for you to come in."

Bernie looked intently at her. The evening had been so perfect and she wanted to treasure its memory by herself. "If you don't mind, I think I'll skip the hot chocolate. Right now, I'm pretty tired and need to call it a night. I do have a date with Grant next Saturday; so, I'll tell you more about him as I discover it."

"That's okay, dear. I understand." Zeva stood up, put her arms around Bernie's shoulders and gave her a big squeeze. "I love you so much."

"Love you too, Nana."

Bernie left the kitchen and started to walk up the stairs to her bedroom. Zeva followed her into the hallway and yelled up at her, "I hope you see more of this young man. So far, he sounds very promising."

Bernie stopped and grinned down at her. "Thank you. I'm looking forward to spending more time with him."

As Nana Zeva walked to her bedroom, she put her hands together and raised them toward Heaven. "Please God. Watch over my Bernie." Then she added, thoughtfully, "And who knows—maybe this cadet can bring her a lot of happiness."

# Chapter 2

The following Wednesday, Grant called Bernie at the bank, promptly at eleven as he had said he would. "Hi Beautiful. Are we still on for Saturday?"

Bernie's heart hammered as she recognized his voice. She was so excited that he had actually called her and she didn't hesitate for an instant before she gave her enthusiastic response. "Yes. And I'll bring a lunch."

"Excellent. I'll pick you up at nine hundred. That's nine o'clock in the morning. The weatherman says no rain in sight for Saturday and the temperature will be in the seventies so you'll probably just need a light jacket." Mischief became apparent in his voice as he added, "As for the lunch, I have something to confess to you, I'm not totally a vegetarian."

Amusement laced Bernie's response. "That's good. Because neither am I. And now, I'm going to have my Nana make us some of her fabulous fried chicken."

"Sounds great. After we visit with my dad, we can stop at a nice quiet park. See you at nine hundred on Saturday then."

"Oh, I'll be ready, Cadet, Sir," Bernie said, breathless with anticipation at seeing him again.

After he picked her up, Grant drove to his father's retirement home. On the way, Bernie discovered that he had his whole future planned in detail. After graduation, he would be a commissioned Second Lieutenant in the US Army. And he hoped that he would eventually work for three or four years at the Pentagon. He was confident that because strategy was his strong point, and with the recommendation of his father's friends, he would have no problem landing a good job there. And always, in the back of his mind were thoughts of continuously getting promoted.

Bernie sat beside him, listening intently, as Grant explained that was just the beginning of his long military career. She soon realized that if she got seriously involved with him, her life would be nothing like she had previously anticipated.

Did she really want her life to be nothing more than that of a wife to a career soldier? What about her personal aspirations to advance in the banking industry? She suddenly became aware that Grant would expect his wife to put aside all her own plans and follow in the direction that he led. A smile tugged at the corners of her mouth, as she thought about the possibility that she might actually become his wife some day.

When she entered Grant's father's room, Bernie was impressed with the pictures hanging on the walls—they were of several presidents and army generals. The senior Younger was sitting in a wheelchair, and wearing army fatigues.

He told Bernie that he had intended to serve in the army as long as he could and eventually follow in his own father's footsteps and reach the rank of General. However, he had fallen out of an army jeep, injured his back and had been forced to take early retirement. Drawling the words in a way that left no doubt how much he cared, he was adamant that Grant continue the family tradition of long service to their country. He added that he hoped that Grant would eventually reach a rank higher than either he or Grant's grandfather had achieved.

Listening to Grant's father ramble on about the military, Bernie realized the saying "like father-like son" was never more appropriate than in the relationship between these two men.

She learned that Grant's father had risen quickly through the ranks of the army and had retired with the rank of Colonel. In fact, he demanded that everyone, even the other residents at the retirement home, address him as "Colonel."

The blood thrummed in her head until it drowned out all else as Bernie decided that the Younger clan was one hundred percent military.

After about an hour, Bernie and Grant said their good-byes to his father and walked to the car. Driving along, neither of them said a word and Bernie became conscious of the fact that she had a lot to learn about this man sitting next to her.

As Grant turned left, they saw a sign nearby that read "State Park." Entering the park, he pulled up beside a secluded shelter which overlooked a quiet lake.

They exited the car and Grant got the picnic lunch that Bernie had brought along, out of the back seat. After they had seated themselves at the picnic table, Bernie turned to Grant and said quietly, "I like your father. He seems really nice."

Grant tilted his head and met her gaze. "Yes. Dad gave me good examples in life and I know that I want to follow in his footsteps. The army life is the only one for me and maybe—one day—for my son." He set his mouth in a tight line. "But now young lady, let's try your Nana's fried chicken."

Bernie removed a table cloth from the picnic basket and covered the table. Then she took out the chicken, potato salad and the sodas. After handing Grant a paper plate and plastic utensils, she moved closer to him.

He reached over, put his arm around her shoulders, and gave her a gentle kiss on the cheek. "I'm very fond of you Bernie. And I hope that this isn't our first and last date. I really want to get to know you. And there's so much that I want to tell you and show you."

Bernie sat silently with a thoughtful look on her face. She reached for a plate and a piece of chicken. After a few moments, she decided that she would just enjoy the moment.

In the following months, Bernie and Grant spent their weekends together because Bernie was busy working every day and Grant was attending classes. And Bernie thought that the weekends with Grant were just glorious. They went out to eat at least once each week-end, and spent most of the time just talking.

Grant had turned Bernie's personal life upside down and her co-workers at the bank could see from the look on her face when she talked about him that she was completely and thoroughly fascinated with him.

"Bernie, I believe that you're falling in love with this fellow," the branch manager, Gale Thomson, told her while they shared a coffee break. Bernie didn't realize it, but Gale was in her second marriage and she understood the difference between infatuation and love. Also, because her first husband had been an army man, she knew that if Bernie decided to marry this military man, her days at the bank would soon be over. Any thoughts that Bernie might have had of having a banking career would go down the drain. Gale also knew that if she tried to advise Bernie to seriously consider the pros and cons of marrying a career military man, it would be in vain. It was impossible to reason with someone who seemed to be so much in love. But then again, Gale told herself—maybe your first love is the one most remembered and cherished.

On Wednesdays, at exactly eleven hundred hours, Grant would call Bernie at the bank. She was always thrilled at the sound of his voice. "Boy, have I got the most wonderful weekend planned, Dear. You are going to enjoy visiting West Point my love, and get a personal tour."

Yes, he called her "Dear" and "my love" regularly now. Her heart fluttered at those words of endearment.

"Will pick you up at 0-nine hundred hours on Saturday," he informed her.

"What should I wear?" Bernie asked.

"Dress casual. No rain is expected and temperature will be in high sixties. Maybe wear a turtle neck sweater, slacks and bring a light jacket," he directed.

"And good walking shoes, I presume?"

"Yes. Our tour should last about two hours. Get ready, lady, you are going to get a big taste of history. And, you might want to bring a thermos of coffee for us."

"Will do." Bernie was prepared to do anything that Grant asked her to do.

After work, Bernie headed home and told Nana of the plans for Saturday. The elderly lady was anxious to hear about Bernie's every move. As Bernie related her morning conversation with Grant, Zeva felt a shiver of apprehension run up her spine. Her granddaughter was clearly smitten with this young man. "Slow down Girl. It sounds like you have hitched your wagon to a rapidly racing comet."

"Oh, do you think that I'm moving too fast?" a somewhat startled Bernie asked.

"Maybe, just a little. But who knows? Your happiness is most important to me and I just want you to be sure that you know what you are doing."

"Nana, I think that I really love Grant. But one thing is for sure; I just can't wait to be with him and I think of him all the time. I feel that he might just be the man that I want to spend the rest of my life with."

Zeva sighed and gazed lovingly at her granddaughter. "Enough said. Help me clean up the kitchen table. Then, you can fold the clothes—the chores never end—even for those in love."


The following morning, Grandma Zeva was still in bed when Bernie entered her bedroom before she left for work. Zeva looked tired and was reluctant to rise.

"It's unusual for you to sleep in so late. Are you feeling well this morning, Nana?"

"I'm okay. Just a little tired."

"Shall I call the doctor?" Bernie asked.

"Don't be silly. Your old granny will feel better after a cup of coffee and a biscuit. You just go on to work."

Bernie looked down at her, a concerned look crossing her face. "Okay. I'll call you about ten and make sure that you're okay."

Zeva nodded. "I'll be awake by then."

Driving to the bank, Bernie's mind was filled with anxiety about both her future and that of her grandmother. She didn't know what her own future was going to be. If she decided to marry and move away who would take care of her grandmother? She knew she would have greater peace of mind if Zeva was settled in a nice retirement home where they would look after her.

And what about her career at the bank? Bernie looked down at the third finger on her left hand. Would she soon be sporting an engagement ring? Nana was certainly right; it appeared as though she was hitching herself to a fast moving comet.

For the remainder of the week, Bernie found that it took her until after midnight each evening to fall asleep. Her mind was in turmoil. She couldn't stop thinking about Grant. And Saturday couldn't come fast enough for her.

# Chapter 3

As the grandfather clock in the hallway chimed nine on Saturday morning, Bernie knew Grant would be at the front door. Before he had a chance to ring the doorbell, Bernie threw the door open. "Looks like we're both on time," she said, giggling. "You look terrific in your dress uniform."

"Thanks." Stepping inside, Grant bent over and gave her a kiss on the cheek. "How's your grandmother this morning?"

"Oh, she's just getting up. I took her breakfast in bed. She's one tough old lady and you can't keep her down."

"Glad to hear that she's doing well," Grant responded politely, before he released a breath. "If you don't mind I would like to get going. It's about a forty five minute ride to the academy from here."

Bernie reached over and pulled her jacket off a nearby chair and picked up a small thermos bag that had been on the chair under the jacket. "I packed a thermos of hot chocolate and a couple of donuts."

Grant grinned down at her. "I'm impressed. You remembered."

"Yes. I remember everything that you tell me." She swept her gaze over him. She added softly, her words thick with emotion, "You like people who follow orders."

He met her eyes and smiled feeling good, really good. "May I reward you?" he asked.

"Yes. Help yourself."

He bent down and kissed her solidly on the mouth.

"If I had known that I was going to get such a nice reward; I would have packed four donuts," Bernie laughed.

He kissed her on the cheek, took the bag from her hands and

propelled her toward the door. "Gotta stay on schedule."

"I always heard that the army runs on time, but, I guess it also runs on its stomach," Bernie said with a grin.

They chatted happily on the way to West Point as they sipped on the hot chocolate and ate the donuts. When they arrived, Grant pulled into the parking lot near the Visitor's Center. As he helped Bernie from the car, Grant looked down at his watch. "We're just in time. There's a ten hundred tour starting now."

"Ten hundred-that's ten a.m.-right?" Bernie asked.

"Yeah. I'm delighted to see that you're starting to understand military time. Every soldier should have that kind of wife." He smiled—a tantalizing little smile.

She drew in a breath and replied soberly. "I think that I might be using military time a lot in the future." She reached into her purse and pulled out a small pad and a pen. "Do I need to take notes during the tour?"

"No. Just enjoy. I'll get you some brochures when we're finished. I hope that you love history; because you are about to get a good dose of it."

A young cadet stepped forward as they entered the building, introduced himself and led them toward a small group of people who were standing near a back wall.

"Before we start the tour, I would like to give you a few facts about West Point," the cadet announced. "President Thomas Jefferson signed legislature establishing the United States Military Academy in 1802. He took this action after ensuring that those attending the Academy would be representative of a democratic society. Colonel Sylvanus Thayer, the 'Father of the Military Academy' served as Superintendent from 1817-1833. He upgraded academic standards, instilled military discipline and emphasized honorable conduct. He put West Point on the map."

Bernie leaned over and whispered to Grant. "I told you that I should take notes."

He gave her a little squeeze. "Don't worry, I'll help you remember all this."

"This way please," the cadet said as he led the group down the hall. Stopping in front of a gallery of photographs of men in military uniforms, he continued, "West Point graduates dominated the highest ranks on both sides during the Civil War. Academy graduates, headed by generals such as Grant, Lee, Sherman and Jackson, set high standards of military leadership for both the North and South."

"Oh, my goodness. I had no idea that all those great men graduated from West Point," an awe-struck Bernie whispered to Grant.

He whispered back. "You can see that I've got some big shoes to fill."

The cadet led the group into the next corridor, where more impressive photos flanked the walls. "Many of you'll recognize these men; Eisenhower, McArthur, Bradley, Arnold, Clark and Patton are among the inspiring array of Academy graduates who met the challenge of leadership in the Second World War."

The tour ended in the commissary, where the cadet said 'good-bye' to the tour group. As Bernie and Grant were ready to leave the building, Grant felt a hand on his shoulder. "Nice to see you in uniform on Saturday, Cadet Younger."

Grant whipped around and saluted the tall gray haired man in full military uniform, with a chest full of ribbons and medals, standing in front of them. "Good morning, Sir."

"Bernie, this is Adjacent General Philip Marks," Grant informed her. "Sir, May I present my friend, Bernadine Hurley."

Bernie gasped. She stared, star struck at the immense array of medals on the General's chest. After a moment, she nervously extended her hand.

The General took her hand in his and gave her a firm handshake. "So nice to meet you."

He turned to Grant. "I'm expecting two gentlemen from the Pentagon on Monday morning and I would like for them to meet you, Cadet Younger. I hope that you will be available to join us about eleven hundred hours?"

Grant took a quick step backwards. He had no idea what the General had in mind. He quickly recovered himself, gave the General a quick salute and said with assurance, "Of course. I'll be there."

After the General walked away, Bernie looked at Grant with pride. "My goodness, Cadet Younger you seem to be very popular with some high profile people."

Grant beamed, linking his arm with hers. "The General served with my father. He's something special. But, now, my dear lady, the second part of your tour begins. And, I am in charge."

"Who else?" Bernie tucked her hand in his. "Lead the way."

"Oh, you'll love our next stop," he said in an excited tone.

He led her outside the building and down to the edge of the Lincoln Hall parking lot. Here a rocky foot trail followed the shoreline of the nearby Hudson River's western bank. A nearby sign read "Visitors must be accompanied by a cadet."

"This trail is West Point's famous 'Flirtation Walk' or as we cadets call it, 'Flirtie'," Grant said, as he guided Bernie along the trail that turned from level to steep and rocky at points. "You can see why I told you to wear sturdy shoes," Grant said as they walked slowly along. "And only cadets and their guests may use the trail."

Bernie looked up at him. "Well, then Sir, I am deeply honored."

As they approached a cement bench next to the trail, Grant reached into his pocket, pulled out a handkerchief and dusted off the bench. He took Bernie's hand and guided her toward the bench. "Please have a seat, Bernie. I have something special that I want to talk to you about."

Bernie sat down and watched with anxiety as Grant paced up and down in front of her. Finally, he stopped pacing. "Do you like football, Bernie?"

"Yes. The school that I graduated from in Syracuse had some good teams. Why?"

He stood directly in front of her and shifted from one foot to the other. "Well, in 1945, West Point had a team that won every game. I have a picture on my wall of two of the greatest players, Doc

Blanchard and Glenn Davis. They beat Navy thirty-two to thirteen."

Bernie scowled and looked at him with disbelief. "Grant, you brought me here to talk football?"

He sighed and took a deep breath. "No. Not really. There's something else I wanted to ask you. Please relax."

"Okay Grant, you're in charge." Bernie could not believe that this usually very decisive man, now seemed to be very hesitant—almost tongue tied. "Well, go ahead. I'm sitting right here." She pulled him down onto the bench beside her.

Grant shifted in his seat. "I can't believe how nervous I am." He gasped for air. "Here goes."

He reached into his pant pocket and pulled out a black velvet box. He snapped it open and pushed it toward Bernie.

Inside the box was a white emerald cut diamond ring. Bernie stared at Grant as her eyes opened widely. She could not believe what she was seeing.

Grant took her hand in his. "Bernie, will you marry me?"

She sat there silent for a long moment. She could not believe the words that she had just heard. Her knight in shining armor, her dream man, wanted to marry her.

"I realize that we've only known each other a short time," Grant said. "But, I am a man of action. I know what I want from life. And right now, I want you. I know that we can have a wonderful future together."

Bernie was hopeful and terrified—nervous. She stared at him and thought for a few moments before answering. Then, deciding that her future lay with this exciting and self assured young man, she shouted, "Yes" and threw her arms around him.

He drew back and with shaking hands took the ring from the box and slipped it onto her finger. Giving her a big kiss, he said,"I'll make you a good husband, I promise."

His simple words tugged at her heart. "I'm sure you will. And I hope that I can be all that you want in a wife."

After kissing passionately for some time, they stood up and resumed their walk. Grant stopped along the way and pointed out a statue of General Sherman and other features on the trail. "I guess that you heard I have an appointment with General Marks on Monday. I have so much I want to talk over with you. Let's head back to the car. We can stop on the way home for supper and then I'll take you home."

Bernie could not stop Grant from talking as they ate their supper at Denny's, outside of Middleton. He was filled with excitement over his plans.

"Here's my or should I say—our future. I will graduate the last Friday in May and I think we should be married on Saturday, the day afterwards. Here, at West Point, there is a beautiful chapel where we can have the ceremony. My parents were married there."

"Oh, that sounds lovely," Bernie replied, anxious to please him. "I really don't attend church much and—well, your chapel will be just fine."

Grant continued, "I'll take care of most of the planning. You'll just have to pick out your wedding gown and choose a bridesmaid or two. My room-mate will be my best man, you know, Cadet Maxwell Turner. I can get the chapel at about eleven hundred on Saturday and reserve a small hall for the reception afterwards."

"So far, that sounds wonderful," Bernie said, almost weak with the speed that all of this was taking place.

"I'll make a list of what duties you need to take care of; like the invitations," Grant said.

"I'll do my part to pull this together," Bernie replied.

"I knew that you were the one the minute that I met you," Grant said confidently. "I've got to call my dad and give him the good news. I'm so glad that we're on the same page about this wedding. Now, let's head for your house so you can tell your Grandma about our plans."

On their way to Bernie's home, both were silent, deep in thought.

They walked hand in hand to the front porch where Grant said, "I'll call you tomorrow night and give you more details about the wedding." He ran out to his car, extremely excited.

Bernie called out to him, "Grant, no kiss good night?"

He raced back to the porch and kissed her ardently. "Sorry. I'm so excited that you said yes. Can't wait to tell the Colonel the good news. God, I love you."

# Chapter 4

The days and weeks flew by after Grant put the engagement ring on Bernie's finger. Bernie had spent some of her time reading wedding magazines where some of the women had told of becoming very nervous and apprehensive about the arrangements for their big day. And, she vowed that she would not allow herself to be like that. She sat back, contented to allow Grant to make the majority of the arrangements. All she had to do was to send out the invitations, purchase her wedding gown and select one for her Maid of Honor, April.

She learned from Grant that the school's chaplain and his wife had guided many couples through weddings at West Point. And they helped Grant with the arrangements for the ceremony, flowers, photographer, invitations and the reception. Bernie thought that most women would love a guy like Grant who seemed to be selecting the best of everything for the occasion.


Now, it was Thursday morning and just days before graduation and the wedding. Grant had made arrangements for Nana, Bernie and April to stay at a hotel near West Point.

Early that morning, on the drive to West Point, while Nana was napping in the back seat, April reluctantly decided to tell Bernie something suspicious that she had observed the week before. One evening, she had spotted Grant at a small restaurant near West Point, dining with a very attractive woman. Sitting very close together, he was holding hands with the tall slender woman with long curly auburn hair. Their heads were almost touching, as they laughed and talked intently. To April's dismay, it appeared that the soon to be married Grant was seriously flirting with the woman. It had taken her days and a lot of consideration before she decided to tell Bernie about it.

Still floating on her heavenly cloud, Bernie dismissed the incident. "That's probably was just an innocent dinner with some girl that Grant has known for a long time. I'm sure he will have a reasonable explanation if I decide to ask him about it."

The three women had arrived promptly at noon on Thursday at the Thayer Hotel as Grant had instructed. He was sitting on a sofa near the reception desk patiently waiting for them.

"Morning ladies," Grant said, as he jumped to his feet and led them over to the sofa. After they were seated he said, "I've already checked you in. Here are the card keys for your rooms."

Pulling a sheet of paper and a couple of envelopes from his briefcase, he handed them to Bernie. "Here's the week end agenda. And here are your invitations and admission cards for the graduation. We graduate at fifteen-hundred on Friday."

Bernie took the envelopes and placed them in her purse. Glancing up shyly at him, she asked, "I'm still your number one girl. Right Grant?"

He glanced away, the lines of his jaw firm, his lips whitened as he momentarily panicked. Then, he regained his composure, but his eyes were cool. "Sure. Why do you ask?"

Bernie could feel her heart start to flutter in her chest. She swallowed and took a deep breath. "Well, April saw you about a week ago having dinner with an attractive girl with auburn hair. She said that the two of you looked very friendly and were deep in conversation." She tried to smile-tried to feel confident about his answer-but at that moment all felt flat.

Grant sat upright, looked over at April and sent her a look sharp enough to sever the nose from her face. "Oh that was just a wedding co-coordinator giving me some ideas about the wedding." He was more than a little annoyed that April had shared her suspicions with

Bernie. He was furious.

Tapping down his anger, he reached over and took Bernie's hands in his, looking deeply into her eyes. "I'm sure you aren't upset about that are you, Bernie?"

She nodded because she wanted to believe him. She forced a small smile into place and replied with some effort, "No. Of course not. I trust you. I'll never doubt your love for me."

"I would hope so." As far as Grant was concerned the subject was now closed. "Now, let's talk about the graduation ceremony."

"We'll be sure to get there in plenty of time," Bernie said, anxious to change the subject. Both Nana and April sat silently by, marveling at how quick Bernie was to believe anything Grant said.

After a few moments, April sighed and said, "We sure are lucky with this nice weather for the third week in May. Thank God, no wind either. My hairdo should hold up for at least two or three days."

Bernie looked at her and smiled, "And it looks great." Then turning to Grant, she added, "I'm going to wear my hair in a simple upsweep for the wedding. That way it will look a little more formal than the way I usually wear it."

Grant's face stiffened and his eyes were cool. He was not at all concerned with how the two ladies were going to wear their hair. He was apprehensive about keeping the whole week end on his strict schedule. "By the way, after the graduation, there will be a small reception. And ladies, I'm confident, that you'll all look nice for both the graduation and the ceremony."


Nana, Bernie and April spent the afternoon, getting settled in their hotel rooms. That evening, they met Grant and Max and the five went out to dinner. After dinner, they returned to the hotel and Nana went up to her room to go to bed, while the other four sat in the piano bar enjoying the music and a couple of drinks.


Friday was the big day for the graduating West Pointers. The cadets filed onto the field of Michie Stadium that had been set with row upon row of chairs for the graduates. Everyone was eager to hear the commencement speech that was to be delivered by the President of the United States.

Nana, Bernie and April were in awe as they watched Cadet Grant Younger and Cadet Maxwell Turner file in with the parade of graduates. Sitting next to Bernie, was Grant's father, who Grant had not expected to attend, because of poor health. And on the other side of April, were Max's parents, who the girls had just met the previous evening.

Watching her future husband graduate from West Point was very thrilling to Bernie. She wrapped her arms around her waist. She was beside herself with excitement.

The commencement lasted almost two hours and when it finished, the whole class of graduates flung their military hats into the air, cheering loudly. Bernie took a photo of Grant tossing his hat into the air and the photo would later hang on the wall where ever Grant and Bernie Younger lived.

After the graduating class was dismissed, Grant rushed over to Bernie. "Thanks for being here, Bernie. I'm still a bit disappointed that my father couldn't come."

A small smile curved her lips. "I've got a surprise for you. Turn around."

Grant whipped around and was astonished to see Colonel Grant Younger II, standing nearby. "Oh, my God, Dad. You made it. I thought your back was giving you excruciating pain."

Colonel Younger grasped his son around the shoulders and shook his hand. "No matter, how much pain I'm suffering, I decided I just had to come. This lovely young lady called me and told me how important this day was to you and I realized that I couldn't miss this and your wedding. She even arranged transportation for me to get here."

Grant turned to Bernie with tears of gratitude in his eyes and gave her a hug. "Thank you, my darling. What a great surprise."

Glancing back at his dad, he added in a firm voice, "Now, you can see why I love this gal so much."

The Colonel nodded. "Yes. I understand. But, now if you and your friends will excuse me, I'm a little tired. I plan to take a cab back to the hotel. I need to save my strength. Tomorrow, at the wedding, I'm escorting your future wife down the aisle."

After lunch with Cadets Turner and Younger and the others, Bernie, April and Nana headed back to the hotel to relax for the remainder of the afternoon.

"See you at the chapel tomorrow, dear," Bernie said to Grant. "I need my rest and well, tomorrow is a big day. And, I'm starting to get very nervous about it."


The wedding was scheduled for eleven in the morning; or, as Grant would say eleven hundred hours. After Nana, dressed in a lovely peach colored lace dress was escorted down the aisle and to her seat, Bernie waited in the back of the chapel for the ceremony to begin. She was dressed in a floor length off-white strapless dress, her hair was done in a simple upsweep with white baby breaths tucked into it and she carried a bouquet of white roses.

Grant's father had agreed to accompany Bernie down the aisle and was splendid looking in his full dress army uniform. April, dressed in a strapless cocktail length baby blue silk dress preceded Bernie down the aisle of the chapel, which was filled with bouquets of white roses and baby breath. The chapel overflowed with Grant's fellow cadets and their families.

Standing at the altar, waiting for the ladies to come down the aisle were Grant and his best man, Max, both in full dress military uniforms. They looked splendid in their short blue jackets and black trousers with yellow stripes. Grant had told Bernie that the uniforms were symbolic of those of the Civil War era.

Bernie felt like she was in a dream. When she glanced shyly up at Grant, her heart begin to beat rapidly in her chest. She could not believe how handsome he was.

A photographer stood behind the men, prepared to take video of the whole ceremony. The thought occurred to Bernie that she must get an extra copies of it made for her Nana and Grant's father.

When the music started, April carrying flowers that matched her gown started down the aisle. Out of the corner of her eye, she could see Bernie's Nana quietly smiling as she wiped the tears that ran down her face. She appeared to be so happy and excited for her lovely granddaughter.

Walking slowly with the aide of a cane, Colonel Younger in full dress uniform, with all his medals displayed, proudly escorted Bernie down the aisle to the waiting men. Colonel Younger put Bernie's hand in Grant's and took a seat nearby.

The ceremony lasted about forty-five minutes and the couple exited the church as a double row of cadets crossed their swords to form an arch for them to walk under. Bernie was beside herself with how Grant had arranged everything. The ceremony was just perfect, she thought. And she later decided that the reception was equally just as wonderful.

Grant had rented a small ballroom at the Thayer Hotel for the sit-down dinner for approximately seventy-five guests. A violin quartet played during the dinner which consisted of a choice of prime rib or grilled salmon, baked potatoes, fresh broccoli and assorted rolls.

Following the dinner, the newly-wed couple cut the three tier cake which was topped by a miniature bride and a groom, in a West Point dress uniform.

After the dinner, April and Max drove back to Middleton with Nana.

By four that afternoon, Second Lieutenant Grant Younger and his wife, were on their way to Niagara Falls for their honeymoon, where they were to spend three days before heading to New York City for several more days.

As they stood looking down at the Falls, Bernie turned to Grant. "I can't believe how you took over the plans for the wedding. Both the graduation and our wedding were just fabulous. Almost out of a story book. And I just love the string of pearls you got me as a wedding gift. That engraved ID bracelet that I gave you, seems so insignificant in comparison."

"Don't say that my love. You gave me the greatest gift of all, surprising me with getting my father to the graduation and then asking him to give you away at the wedding. He was so impressed with you."

"And, I with him. He seems to be a wonderful man. And the wedding and honeymoon seem like a fairy tale to me," Bernie said, looking up at Grant adoringly.

He smiled down at her and drew her close to his side. "And I hope that it will never end."

Shortly after they returned from their honeymoon, 2nd Lt. Grant Younger received his assignment. He would lead a platoon, consisting of two or more squads and containing sixteen to forty-four soldiers at Fort Dix, southeast of Trenton, New Jersey.

Bernie was upset that she had to leave her Grandmother, but was confident that a near-by neighbor would look in on her regularly.

Bernie had given up her job at the bank when she got married and moved away. The Younger's were to stay at Ft. Dix for four years. While in Ft. Dix, Grant got her a part time job at the commissary. During this time, Grandma Zeva passed away and Bernie returned home for the funeral. Grant could not get away from his duties so he did not accompany her.

Within a short time, Bernie learned that Grant's job was always of the greatest concern to him and he was constantly working to reach the next rank.

# Chapter 5

After only three months into their marriage and their stay at Ft. Dix, it was clear to Bernie that 2$^{nd}$ Lt. Grant Younger had only two goals dominating his mind. His first was to make 1$^{st}$ Lieutenant as quickly as possible. That, Bernie discovered would take about eighteen months to achieve. After that, Grant was anxious to obtain the rank of Captain. Grant was constantly seeking more prestige, more money and a better lifestyle for them, he said. But Bernie realized that he was all about the army.

Grant's second goal was dependent on Bernie. He wanted desperately for her to bless him with a son—a big healthy son. As the months passed and she learned that getting pregnant was not easy, Bernie grew more and more desperate.

She also discovered that due to his extreme dedication to his career, Grant's job was not just nine to five. At least two days a week and sometimes for days at a time, Grant would stay on base, busy with meetings and field trips. As time passed by, Bernie found herself becoming more and more desperate and lonely.

Fortunately, they had been able to find a very comfortable apartment. When Grant was home he would ask Bernie, "Are you feeling okay?" After a couple of months, she saw the hopelessness in his expression as he asked, "Aren't you pregnant yet? When am I going to get my son?" Then as he strolled angrily away from her, he stopped short, his eyes threatening as he added sternly, "Don't let me down."

Bernie quickly learned that Grant did not like to hear excuses about anything so she would just take a step backward, hang her head and answer, "Soon, I hope." She sounded both embarrassed and apologetic as her devastation over the situation continued.

Her days were spent mostly in the apartment, except for those hours that she spent working part-time at the PX on base, as a cashier. This was her only social outlet, and at times, she felt like she was living in a prison.

Once in a while, on Saturday night, Grant would take her out to dinner in the near-by town. On these occasions, Bernie would dress all up, and Grant would be out of uniform, wearing jeans, a sport shirt and loafers. When he was around the house, he would live in his fatigues.

The two bedroom apartment was sparse, but comfortable. With people living closely on both sides of them and the walls paper thin, the atmosphere was not very romantic. Bernie thought that it was no wonder she had difficulty becoming pregnant, because she could never quite seem to relax during their hurried love-making. She was rapidly becoming frustrated over her situation, as was Grant. It was the sullen, closed-off expression in his eyes that always got her attention. She knew what that meant. He was going to find fault with everything she did. She braced herself daily for a barrage of complaints. Was her dream man changing? Maybe she had never seen the real Grant Younger until now.

Grant's world was centered on the army and the army was everything to him. In the back bedroom closet, he kept a complete set of dress uniforms with medals, fatigues and combat boots. All of these were custom tailored to fit. Grant was determined to always look sharp when in uniform.

The one bright note in Bernie's life had been the lovely friend that she had found in her next door neighbor, Joy Comfort.

Joy's husband, Captain Jack Comfort, worked in the same building as Grant and the four became close friends. Occasionally, Bernie and Joy would take turns having morning coffee in each other's kitchen.

At least twice a month, the two couples would get together to play Mah Jong. Grant loved this game because he usually won.

With Joy, Bernie felt like she was looking into a mirror where she saw a reflection of her own frustration with the army life. Both of their husbands were dedicated army men and spent most of their time concentrating on their careers. Bernie and Joy made it a point to not talk much about their husband's commitment to the service. And Joy also seemed depressed much of the time, as was Bernie.

Lately, Bernie had started to feel...a little...well, "cheated," was probably the right word about her life. Grant had made his wishes clear and she was always afraid to go against him in any matter. That's the marriage that you have. Stop, wasting your time, thinking about it. But, then, she would shrug her shoulders and tell herself, "Things will be different for Grant and me once our child is born. And please Lord, make it a boy."

The last few weeks had taken a toll on Bernie. Her face was drawn and tired-looking, the expression in her eyes, sad, almost haunted. This particular morning, Joy lent Bernie the use of her car so she could go to the license bureau to get her driver's license renewed. Then she got a passport, in case Grant got assigned overseas. Finally, she headed over to see Dr. Sue Stark, her gynecologist. If Bernie's suspicion was right; it would be good news for Grant, her and their marriage.

Bernie arrived at the doctor's office early for her one o'clock appointment, since it was right across the street from the license bureau. The receptionist looked up, saw Bernie, and said, "The doctor is ahead on her appointments today. We can take you right in."

Bernie sat in the small room, waiting for the doctor to enter, and noticed the doctor's certificate on the wall. Dr. Sue Stark had graduated from Ohio State and had done her internship at a medical college in Toledo, Ohio.

"Now, Mrs. Younger, give me an up-to-date account on how you're feeling," the doctor said as she entered the room. After discussing her symptoms and a brief examination, Dr. Sue confirmed that Bernie Younger was indeed, pregnant.

Unexpected tears stung Bernie's eyes and she blinked them back. She felt good, really good, for the first time in months. She was grateful for life, grateful to be here, to be in this moment. "I can't wait to tell my husband, he'll be so excited," Bernie exclaimed as she left the doctor's office.

Knowing that Joy was not expecting her car back soon, Bernie decided to head onto the base and tell Grant the good news in person.

She arrived at the gate and flashed her identity card to the guard stationed there, then drove to her husband's office, parked the car and ran excitedly into his office.

Grant's aide looked up when he saw Bernie rush in. "Good afternoon, Mrs. Younger. Are you here to see your husband?"

"Yes. But, for only a minute," Bernie exclaimed.

"Well, he's in a very important meeting and I doubt if he'd want to be disturbed."

"For this, he will. What I've got to tell him, he must know at once," Bernie answered with a flushed face.

The aide stood up looking very concerned. "Well, okay." He walked over to the office door and knocked gently. A young man, whose stripes indicated that he was a sergeant opened the door and peered out.

"Oh, Sergeant. It's Mrs. Younger and she says that she must see Lt. Younger at once."

Hearing this, Grant jumped up from his desk, rushed to the door and pulled Bernie inside his office. At first, he appeared to be somewhat furious at the interruption, but the tears flowing down Bernie's face momentarily frightened him. He put his arm around her and drew her into the room. "You're crying. What's wrong Honey? You're really scaring me."

She smiled serenely up at him and whispered softly, "Oh no, Grant, these are tears of joy. I have good news." She lifted her glowing damp eyes-damp with happiness.

Noticing Colonel Blake sitting in front of Grant's desk, she added, "I'm sorry to have interrupted you, Sir. But, I had some news that I just had to share with my husband and it couldn't wait until he got home."

"Of course. I understand," the Colonel said. He stood up and walked over to them.

Grant looked down at her. "Tell me, please."

"You're going to be a father," she whispered.

Grant drew in a deep breath. His eyes suddenly filled with gladness. "You're positive?" This was the news that he had been waiting to hear for months.

"I just came from the doctor's. We're going to have a baby in about seven months."

He whirled around. "You hear that Colonel, I'm going to be a father." His voice was filled with tears as he asked, "A boy right?"

"It's too soon to know," Bernie answered with a dazzling smile.

He was indignant. "It's got to be a boy."

The Colonel grabbed Grant's hand and shook it vigorously. "Well, congratulations, to both of you." He smiled down at Bernie and let out a small chuckle. "But, we do have women in the army."

"I know. But I'm certain it will be a boy," Bernie said with great conviction. "And, I'm sorry I interrupted your meeting, Sir."

"No problem. Right now, Lt. Younger, you should take this young woman out and celebrate. That's an order. We can resume this meeting tomorrow at eleven hundred hours."

"Yes, Sir," Grant replied, smiling broadly, as he drew his wife to his side and gave her a big squeeze.

Hopefully, this will bring us closer than we have been for the past several months, Bernie thought. Her heart was almost bursting with happiness.

# Chapter 6

After she had fulfilled the first part of Grant's dream for a son, by finally becoming pregnant, Bernie had hoped that maybe a renewed love life would occur between them.

However, gaining rank seemed to be constantly foremost on Grant's mind. He felt that he had to put in long hours on duty and constantly chum with the top brass to achieve that goal. Having recently been appointed to the rank of 1$^{st}$ Lieutenant was not enough for him and he was now striving to acquire Captain's bars.

Only on week-ends did Grant and Bernie spend any significant amount of time together. In the evenings, Grant would watch sports on television, looking up only occasionally to ask Bernie how she was feeling and how her pregnancy was progressing. At his coldness, Bernie's eyes would fill with tears. Her face crumpled with pain. It only lasted for a few seconds, then she regained control, blinked away the tears, filled her face with a smile and answered him cheerfully, "Oh, everything is fine."

Anxious to learn whether the expected baby was to be a boy or girl, Grant made it a point to accompany Bernie to her doctor's appointment with Dr. Sue during her fourth month for a sonogram.

Grant sat beside the table that Bernie was lying on, as Dr. Sue, with a nurse standing beside her, conducted the test. Before he had a chance to ask the sex of the baby, the doctor announced, "Well, Lt. Younger, you're a lucky man, your wife is going to give birth to a boy."

Grant smiled an utterly maddening, arrogant smile and jumped to his feet. "Yes. Yes." Then he turned to the doctor, "You're sure?"

"Yes. I'm positive. I saw his little plumbing." She dismissed a breath in a disgusted rush.

Grant thumped her on the back and clasping her hand, added, "Make sure that you give my wife the necessary instructions to complete her pregnancy in good condition."

Dr. Sue's lip's lifted with a mocking smirk. "I can assure you, Lieutenant that your wife and I will be on the same page."

The nurse helped Bernie to her feet as Dr. Sue started to leave the room. She turned around and glanced at Bernie, with compassion. "My nurse will schedule your next appointment, Mrs. Younger."

"Thank you for the good news," Bernie answered as she let out a relieved breath. In her mind, she was quietly thanking God for the news that she was to have a son. She knew that Grant would have been filled with impotent rage if the baby had been a girl. It was important to him to carry on the Younger line and West Point tradition.


For the next few months, Grant took extremely good care of Bernie. He made sure she stayed close to home after she stopped working and that she followed the doctor's instructions to the tee. When he didn't stay overnight at the base, Grant made it a point of sleeping in the back bedroom. He had decided that sexual relations with Bernie might harm the child. And Bernie didn't need to look in a mirror to know that with her swollen body, that she was unappealing sexually to him.

On the nights that he spent at the base, Grant stayed in the Bachelor's Quarters, where he occasionally enjoyed the company of one of the female officers.


After the birth of the baby, Dr. Sue informed the couple that Bernie had an extremely difficult delivery and suggested she not have any more children. That statement made the couple's already strained relationship even more difficult.

Grant decided that Bernie was to be strictly a stay-at-home

mother and he expected her to expose his son to books, crafts and a thorough exercise program as soon as he was old enough to participate in them. The boy's future was to follow in the Younger tradition, a soldier through and through, right from the beginning.

Bernie was ordered to raise Grant Younger IV, in the image of his father and fearing the wrath of her strict husband, she reluctantly did so. Right from the start, the young boy learned that he was expected to fulfill his father's wishes and follow in his military footsteps.


When young Grant was in the fifth grade, his father reached the rank of Captain and was transferred to Baden Baden, Germany. Forcing a smile to her face, Bernie packed up their belongings and the young boy and moved overseas to the new base.

In the months that followed, Grant decided that living in Europe would broaden young Grant's view of the world. But once again, Bernie was ordered to stay at home and focus all her attention on raising the boy. At Grant's insistence, he was enrolled in a military grade school in Germany.

While Bernie was a wonderful and caring mother to young Grant, she never seemed to have the opportunity to really bond with him. Consequently, she received little affection from either her husband or son.

Blocking out her feelings of hurt, Bernie was forced to wait at home while Grant took his son on week-end trips to London and Paris and other sites around Europe. She knew that her husband was shallow and she often flinched at his continued abruptness, but, once again, she wrapped herself in the belief that her life would improve in the near future.

Sometimes Bernie simmered with indignation, but she continued with her simple life of being a stay-at-home mom until Grant finally permitted her to obtain a part time job at the local military base. Things looked a little brighter for her after that as she welcomed the opportunity to get out and meet other people.

The four year tour of Germany seemed long to Bernie and

winters in Germany were brutal. But, Grant eventually reached the rank of Major and added several more medals and ribbons to his chest. While Bernie was personally unhappy, her son was thriving and her husband seemed to be fulfilling his potential.


After his tour in Germany, Major Grant Younger was re-assigned to Fort Lee, New Jersey. Young Grant was now ready to enter high school and his father enrolled him in a private all-male military high school.

The family had just gotten settled into their new lives in New Jersey, when Grant accepted a four year tour to Iraq. When she heard this, Bernie said nothing, and then let out a frustrated breath. She had still been hoping that their private life would improve. Grant, on the other hand, lifted his chest arrogantly and said, "This assignment will give me the opportunity to make the rank of Lt. Colonel."

Now, with her husband serving overseas, Bernie jumped at the opportunity to obtain a full-time job at a local bank. It was what she had trained for years ago. Even though her life was still lonely, it was better than it had been in the previous years. She realized her husband didn't much care what she did or what she thought. Grant always lived life as he desired.

As time went on, her job at the bank continued to become more important and fulfilling to Bernie. Young Grant was now in his senior year in high school and was tops in his class. Both he and his father were convinced that he would eventually be admitted to West Point.

With Grant Senior on duty overseas and young Grant, busy in school, there was not much interaction between the two of them and Bernie.

Young Grant even stayed at school during the holiday vacations and the summer. His father would call him at least once a week to see how he was doing in school. Occasionally, when Grant was on leave, he would fly home and spend time with his son, helping him to plan his future at West Point.

Bernie could easily see that her son's future was mapped out before him, thanks to her husband. And she had no say in it.

Then, almost two months before young Grant was due to graduate from high school, Bernie received tragic news. At six in the morning, the door bell at her apartment rang.

As Bernie tried to rouse herself from a deep sleep, she heard persistent thumping on the door. Finally, she climbed slowly out of bed. After putting on her robe and slippers, she made her way to the front door.

Looking through the peep hole, she recognized a uniformed male with the eagles insignia of a Colonel and a female Lieutenant, both of whom she didn't know. Bernie slowly opened the door, a feeling of cold premonition gripping her.

"Mrs. Younger. I'm Colonel Simpson and this is Lt. Jones. We need to speak with you. May we come in?"

Bernie backed up and signaled for them to enter the room. The Colonel took Bernie gently by the arm and guided her toward the sofa. "Please sit down, Mrs. Younger."

Her knees now shaking, Bernie did as she was instructed. The female officer sat down beside her and took Bernie's hands in hers. The Colonel stood solemnly in front of the women.

After removing his hat, he said with a slight quiver in his voice, "I've got some sad news for you, Mrs. Younger. We just received the news that Major Younger and his aide were killed yesterday in an explosion. While driving through a bomb infested field, they ran over a land mine and were both instantly killed."

Bernie looked up at the Colonel and then looked over at the female officer. At first, her mind could not seem to comprehend what she had just heard. She never flinched or cried. She remained serene. She sat there silently for a few moments and when the news finally sank in— it was as if a gray cloud had descended around her, blocking out everything else. With tears threatening to fill her eyes, she asked, "Are you sure it was Grant? I can't believe it." With her heart pounding and tears starting to flow, she put her head down and covered her face with her hands.

The Colonel sat down on the other side of her and placed his hat on the coffee table. "Yes. I'm sure. The war department confirmed it. But, if it is any consolation, Major Younger did give his life for his country. He was an excellent soldier and was soon to become a Lt. Colonel and be assigned to the Pentagon."

Bernie sat back in her seat, as desolation filled her heart. Tears streamed down her cheeks and she stared blankly at the officers. "Imagine—the Pentagon and a Colonel—both of those were always Grant's ultimate dreams."

She sat silently for a few moments, completely unsure of what to do or say. Suddenly, her mind cleared a little. "Oh my gosh, I've got to call my son and tell him this tragic news."

"Don't worry yourself, Mrs. Younger. A member of the army is also giving your son this news, as we speak. All the arrangements for bringing Major Younger back to the States have been made."

With an instinctive need to pull herself together, Bernie glanced at him. "Thank you. A nice military funeral would be Grant's wish."

"I understand that Major Younger wanted to be buried at Arlington Cemetery?" the Colonel asked.

Her eyes full of sorrow, she answered calmly, forcing a faint smile to her face, "Yes. But, I'm stunned at this news."

"I empathize with you. I'll order my office to start making the arrangements. Once Major Younger is back in the States, we can set the date and time for the funeral and burial."

"Thank you."

"My office will contact you in the next couple of days with the final arrangements. The government, will, of course, take care of all the expenses related to the funeral and burial."

Bernie was now sobbing quietly and the female officer handed her a handful of tissues. She patted Bernie's hand. "I knew Major Younger briefly. You were so fortunate to have been married to such a wonderful military man. And, I'm certain that he was also a loving and faithful husband."

Bernie did not know how to respond to this statement. After all; Grant was anything but loving and faithful. She rubbed her arms, chilled now—chilled to the bone.

The Colonel and his aide, stood up. "Now, we'll take our leave." He reached into his pocket and pulled out a card. "We'll call you as soon as we have further information. In the meantime, here's my number. If you have any questions or concerns after you talk to your son, please feel free to give me a call."

"Thank you for being so kind. My son and I are very appreciative."

After they left the apartment, Bernie sat silently on the sofa. "No. No. Grant can't be gone," she croaked, as she wrapped her arms around herself and rocked back and forth, trying to deny the undeniable. "No. Oh, no." She could not believe that her husband was suddenly gone—gone forever.

# Chapter 7

After Colonel Simpson left the apartment, Bernie sat motionless, staring into space and feeling helpless. Her body was stiff from shock. Her mind was traveling a mile a minute and her heart was pounding very rapidly. She drew in a huge, shuddering gasp of pain, her eyes still filled with tears. Finally, she managed to pull herself together and re-group her thoughts. Reality hit her—at last she comprehended what she had just heard—she would never see her husband again.

She dragged herself up from the sofa and slowly walked into the kitchen to make a cup of coffee. What will I do next, she thought.

There was a rumor that the bank where Bernie worked would be bought out and she might be laid off from her job. And now this. A wave of desperation and hopelessness over took her. Finally, she decided that she must pull herself together for the sake of her son.

Maybe, she should take Joy up on her offer to attend church services once again. Bernie had fallen away from her religion, but now the thought of returning to it, gave her a glimmer of hope. After all, the marriage to Grant had been in name only for the last few years. There had been no true love between them anymore. But, what about their son? Young Grant had always been her husband's boy and his whole life had been planned out. And there seemed to have been no place for Bernie in it.

She drew in a deep breath, her eyes were red and swollen. She realized that her son, yes, her son, would need her now. What to do? She told herself to slow down. Perhaps, it was time for her to take back her life. First, I should call Grant. Yes. Call him.

The sound of the phone ringing brought Bernie out of her deep thoughts. Taking her cup of coffee with her, she walked into the living room, put the coffee cup down on a small end table and sat down on the nearby chair. "Hello," she said in a strained voice.

"Mom. It's Grant. I just received a call about Dad. They said that he was killed by a land mine." His quivering voice told Bernie how upset he was.

She sat back, her heart pounding. He had called her "Mom" and seemed to be reaching out to her for comfort. It had been many years since he had turned to her. She took a deep breath as she tried to figure out how she could ease his pain.

I've got to be strong, she decided. She paused, struggling for the right words. Her boy needed her and she softly answered, "I know Son. Colonel Simpson and his aide were just here to break the news to me. But, they said that your father died a hero and in the line of duty. Also, he was killed instantly and did not suffer. We have to take comfort in this."

"I guess you're right; but, it's so hard to believe that Dad is just suddenly gone forever," Grant sobbed.

"I'm in shock too, Son, but, he's not really gone—he will always be in our hearts. And we must pray for him now," Bernie replied gently, as she blinked back the rush of emotions.   Little did young Grant know how loveless her life with her husband had really been.

She straightened her shoulders and inhaled a deep breath, willing away her sorrow. "Would you like to come home and stay with me until after your father's funeral?" she added with heartfelt sympathy in her voice. She realized that her husband's sudden death was an agonizing loss for their son.

"Thanks, but I can't. I haven't been feeling so hot lately and I've gotten behind on some of my classes. The lady who talked to me about the arrangements for Dad said that they would fly his body back to the States in a couple of days. She said that the funeral would be scheduled in about a week at Arlington Cemetery. So, I'll join you there," Grant said.

"I could really use your shoulder to lean on for the next few days.

However, I think you're right, your studies should come first." She paused for a moment and heaved in a breath. "That's what your father would have wanted." Then, she added sadly, "I do miss you."

After a long pause, Grant whispered back, "And I miss you too, Mom. But right now I need to get some rest. Then, I have to decide what my next step will be after I finish school. I'll call you when we know the exact date and time of the funeral."

"Good. Talk to you then. And take care," Bernie said as she hung up the phone. She decided not to question her son about his future. Maybe, he's not planning to attend West Point like his father wanted, she thought.

She sat in the living room with her head held low. She could hardly think. She felt as if a ton of bricks was weighing her down, dragging her into an emotional abyss. Then anger began to build in her, a hot penetrating wrath that seeped through her veins and spread like quicksand. Her mouth firmed into a taut line as she fought to control it. It wasn't fair that her son's father had been taken away from him.

She was trying to calm herself down, when the doorbell rang. She slowly got to her feet, lumbered across the room and opened the door to find Joy Comfort standing in front of her.

Struggling to keep her emotions in check, Joy rushed through the doorway and threw her arms around Bernie. "Oh Bernie, I'm so sorry. I just heard the news about Grant."

The agony of Grant's death had plunged deep into Bernie's soul. She took a step back, took a tissue from her pocket and wiped her eyes. "Yes, two soldiers from Fort Lee just came with the news. Needless to say, I'm just stunned. I can't believe that this happened. I always thought that Grant was invincible. Nothing could happen to him." A sob burst from her as her knees started to buckle.

Joy put her arms around her. Bernie wiped her tears and desperation edged her words as she whispered, "Colonel Simpson said that it was a land mine and that both Grant and his driver were killed instantly."

"I know. Jack called me with the news." Her voice deepened with sympathy for her friend. "You just have to hang on girl for the sake of your son. He'll need you very much in the next few weeks."

Bernie met her eyes as she tried to think straight. "Yes. I just talked to him and he's been under the weather lately and this news seems to have affected him deeply. He loved his father very much."

"Is he coming home now?" Joy asked.

"No. He said that he wanted to stay at school and catch up on his studies. Said he would meet me at Arlington Cemetery for the funeral. I'm supposed to fly to D.C. I don't know the arrangements for the funeral yet. The Colonel's office was going to contact me with the details."

"You can count on Jack and me accompanying you to the funeral." Joy's eyes were filled with compassion.

Suddenly very tired, Bernie, asked, "Want a cup of coffee, Joy?"

"No. Let's plan on getting together tomorrow morning for it."

"Yes. I would like that," Bernie responded. "I've got to concentrate on getting regrouped."

Following a long and comforting talk with Joy, Bernie felt a little better. After her friend left, Bernie paced around the house, trying not to think too much of the past years with Grant, but, everywhere she turned, something reminded her of him.

For the next two days, she waited anxiously for the call. Finally, the Colonel's office called to tell her the details about the funeral and to make arrangements for a couple of his men to pick up Grant's military gear.

From that point onward, Bernie decided that she had to start making plans for her future. She called Joy. "I finally got some news about Grant's funeral. Is it okay if I run over to your house now and tell you what I know?"

"Sure."

Immediately following their conversation, Joy called her husband and relayed the information to him. "Tell Bernie to come over for supper," he replied. "I'm going to make a couple of calls now and we'll all talk later."

"Got it, dear."

Joy hung up the phone, invited Bernie to supper and asked her what her plans were for the following day.

"I wanted to ask you if you could help me look for a car. It's time that I had transportation," Bernie said, taking command of her situation. "As you know, Grant didn't want me to buy a car and I had been walking to work or else taking a bus. Do you know of any good places to look for a car?"

"Sure my cousin works at the Toyota dealership just outside the base. I'm sure he can help you get a good deal. He's sold cars to lots of the servicemen on the base. I'll take you there in the morning. And there's an insurance agency right across the street from the dealership where you can purchase auto insurance."

By early afternoon, Bernie was the owner of a new teal green Toyota Camry. It was easier than she thought to complete the deal, sign the papers, and get the car insured—and all without the assistance of her husband. She even had her son put on the insurance so that he could drive the car.

Bernie was proud of herself, as she thought. First car of my own. And I can't believe that I purchased it all by myself with the money I saved from working at the bank. And I didn't even need to take out a loan on it.

Later that afternoon, two army officers pulled up to the Younger apartment in a large van, parked it in the driveway, walked up to the front door, and rang the bell.

"Mrs. Younger, we're from Colonel Simpson's office. I believe that you were told to expect us. We are here to pick up your husband's military equipment."

His outstretched hand was ignored by Bernie. She didn't return the greeting. Just, whirled around and headed down the hall. "Yes. The Colonel's secretary told me to expect you. Please follow me."

They followed her down the hallway to the back bedroom. Her legs felt like lead. It felt as if she was walking through mud, as she walked across the room and opened the closet door. "Here's the army issued equipment, and some of his other stuff. I put aside a couple of his medals for his son, but I want you to take the rest of them."

"Thank you," one of the men said as he reached inside the closet to get the equipment. "A new building is being erected on the base, to commemorate the fallen heroes from this base. I'm sure that Major Younger's picture and medals will share a large place in the exhibit."

"Thank you," Bernie said. Her teeth clenched and a muscle worked in the corner of her eye. Her guts turned sour and she thought that she might be sick. "I'm certain that Grant would have been honored to have a prominent place in your exhibit."

The second officer picked up the box of medals from the top of the dresser. Turning to leave the room, he said, "I hope that I can live to be as fine a soldier as your husband was, Mrs. Younger. I knew him quite well and he often talked of how someday his son would follow in his footsteps."

Bernie stared solemnly at him. Now fear that her son would follow in his father's footsteps coiled deep in the middle of her. She didn't want to lose him to a war also.


That evening, at the supper table, Captain Jack Comfort told Bernie plans that he had made for them on the day of the funeral. He had arranged for a car to pick the three of them up and transport them to the airport. From there a military helicopter would transport them to the D.C. air base, where a military car would meet them and take them to Arlington Cemetery. The process would be reversed on the way home after the ceremonies.

'I like that," Bernie said simply. "I'll call my son and tell him the arrangements. He plans to meet us at the cemetery."

After supper, Bernie thanked them for the lovely meal and headed home to call Grant.

"How, are you feeling, Son," she asked after he answered the phone.

"So. So," he responded. "Right now, I'm saving my strength and just concentrating on getting through the funeral. I'll meet you in D.C."

# Chapter 8

Bernie spent the two days before the funeral preparing for it. She had purchased a tailored Talbot suit to wear to the funeral. It was black with white piping around the collar and the sleeves. The sales clerk said it would look very suitable for the occasion with black suede pumps and a black leather handbag. She completed the outfit with a small black hat the clerk recommended. It had a short black veil that would just reach down to her nose and cover her eyes. Bernie decided that the veil would be appropriate because it would hide the dark shadows under her eyes and the probable stream of tears during the ceremony.

She was still numb with shock over the death of her husband but as each hour passed she managed to pull herself together, little by little. "You're on your own now girl," she told herself.

The day before the funeral, Bernie scheduled an appointment for a physical check up with their family physician at the base, Dr. James. She had decided she would probably leave Ft. Lee after she had taken care of personal matters and she wanted a complete physical before she left.

Where she would move to from Ft. Lee would depend on her son's plans after graduation. She wanted to be near him in the future and he had hinted that he was considering moving to California. Slowly, Bernie was starting to think about her future, even though her heart wasn't really into it.

The sky was very overcast the day of the funeral; however, Bernie was grateful that her dear friends, Jack and Joy Comfort were accompanying her to Washington. The government had made all the transportation arrangements for them.

Captain Comfort and Joy, together with a military escort picked Bernie up early on the morning of the funeral. Bernie was shocked at how shaky her voice was when she greeted them. They were driven to a nearby tarmac where an army helicopter was waiting to fly them to Arlington.

Before boarding the special US Army helicopter, Jack introduced Bernie and Joy to the pilot. "This is Major Sam Mercury. We've been friends for years."

"Good morning, ladies. Now, if you will step inside the copter and buckle up we'll be on our way," Sam said with a quick salute.

The Major and Jack Comfort reminisced for a few moments before they took their places in the front seats of the helicopter.

The Major turned around in his seat and addressed Bernie. "Now, Mrs. Younger our next stop will be Arlington Cemetery. This baby moves fast so be sure to fasten your seat belts tight. Our only problem this morning is that a storm is heading toward that region later in the day. So, I'm sorry to say that the quick tour of Arlington that I was going to give you after Major Younger's funeral will have to be put off for another day."

After he was sure that his passengers were secure, Major Mercury fired up the copter and quickly rose into the sky. On the way, he continued talking to his three passengers who were all wearing ear phones.

"I understand that this will be the first time that both of you ladies have ever seen Arlington. So, I would like to tell you a little about it before we arrive there."

Bernie and Joy nodded as they listened intently.

"Well, here goes. Arlington Cemetery covers six hundred and twenty four acres and lies across the Potomac River from Washington, D.C. Major Younger will be buried alongside some of our country's most famous people. Among them are Audie Murphy, a World War II hero and later a movie star. Of course, President John F. Kennedy, George Marshall, Glen Miller, and General George Patton. Well, it's a who's who of famous people to say the least. And I have learned that to honor your husband, he will be buried in a beautiful bronze casket. His ceremony will feature a bugler who will play taps and, of course, an honor guard will fire their weapons in salute. The NCOIC and an army chaplain will perform the ceremony. After the ceremony, you'll be given the flag that covered Grant's casket."

"That sounds just wonderful," Bernie said. "My son and I will be greatly honored."

Major Mercury continued, as he started to change his flight pattern. "I'm a West Point graduate myself and I hope to one day have an illustrious a career as Major Younger did."

Jack Comfort nodded his head. "Yes. Grant was one great soldier. He was due to become a Lt. Colonel next year."

"I heard that," Major Mercury said. He looked over his shoulder at Bernie. "You must be proud that your son might follow in his father's footsteps."

Bernie sat silently, gazing out the window. She realized, at this point, she didn't know what her son's future was to be.

"Finally," Major Mercury continued, "As I mentioned before, we will whisk you right back to the helicopter after the ceremony in order to avoid the inclement weather that is expected to approach the area with several inches of rain."

He nodded his head toward a folder at his side. "Before I leave you after our return trip, I have a folder here that I want to give you. It lists all the attractions that you might want to visit should you return to Arlington sometime later to visit Major Younger's gravesite. You might wish to see notable gravesites and the Memorial Arboretum and Horticulture."

Bernie merely nodded her head. She was suddenly overwhelmed by a mindless, wordless, bottomless lonely feeling.

When they arrived at the cemetery, a military guard led Bernie, Joy and Jack, to the tent that had been set up near the grave site. They were directed to the front row of seats. Shortly after they were seated, young Grant arrived, splendid in his school military uniform. Bernie felt an icy hand clutch at her stomach when she saw her son. Thankful that she had worn the short veil, she closed her eyes and tried to fight back the rush of tears that threatened to claim her.

As Grant hugged her, she let his embrace surround her, let her heart have a moment of peace. Then, Grant turned to introduce the cadet who was accompanying him. "Mom, this is Craig, one of my class mates. He drove me down since I wasn't feeling so good." Her voice quivered as she greeted the young man.

Grant sat down beside his mother, and Craig sat on the other side of him. Grant bent down and kissed Bernie on the cheek. "Good to see you, Mom. Boy, you really look nice."

Somehow, she found the strength to smile at him, drinking in the love in his eyes and the concern in his voice. "Thank you. And so do you. How are you feeling now?"

"Not so hot," he sighed, a rippling sound, ending with a little sob. "We're heading right back to school after the funeral. It's only a month until graduation and I'll have to push hard in order to ace those exams."

Anxious about her son's health, Bernie's eyes filled again with tears, but then she visibly brought herself under control. She was disappointed her son and she had spent so little time together in the past years; however, she was glad to have him at her side during the services. They sat still for a long moment and shared the silence, a heavy kind of silence that grew more and more oppressive until the services began. After the ceremony and the gun salute, Bernie was presented the flag that had covered Grant's coffin.

With Joy's assistance, Bernie stood up and bade a sad farewell to her son and his friend. Then, Captain Comfort escorted his wife and Bernie to the military escort that was going to accompany them back to the waiting helicopter. As the copter started to lift off, the skies darkened and a light rain started to fall. "Good-bye Grant," Bernie said silently, letting her head fall back against the seat. Taking a deep breath, she closed her eyes. The weather matched her darkened spirits. But it was a touching ceremony.

Once back home, the military car drove them back to their apartment complex.

Later, as Bernie sat in her living room, the sky let loose and dumped several inches of rain within a couple of hours. She felt alone and depressed as if someone had dumped ice water on her head. Her stomach was churning and she decided that all she would be able to handle for supper would be a small bowl of soup and some saltine crackers.

Her mind started to revolve about the happenings of the last several days and her son's future. What did Grant have planned after he graduated? Would he be off to California? Or would he follow his father's wishes and head to West Point? Some of her shakiness dissolved, leaving her irritated. And what should I do? Should I follow him wherever he goes and make an attempt to get closer to him? And what didn't Grant tell me about his health?

Her thoughts were interrupted by the ringing of her phone. "Hello. Hello. It's Bernadine Younger."

A voice answered, "Hi, Mrs. Younger. It's Dr. James." His sharp tone penetrated Bernie's thoughts.

"Hi. Hope you got good news on my recent physical." Bernie tucked away her irritation and forced a pleasant ring into her voice.

"Well, the news is good; only it's too much to talk about over the phone. And I have a favor to ask of you. Can you please come in at eight thirty tomorrow morning instead of the scheduled time of one p.m.?"

"Sure. I'll be there." She felt an instinctive need to build her defensive barriers—it was now high in her self-protection.

"And Mrs. Younger, I will have copies of all your records for you. You did say that you were considering moving and you will need them for your new doctor."

"Thank you. I'll see you at eight thirty," Bernie said, as she hung up the phone. She was thankful that one of the perks of Grant's being in the military, was that she had survivor coverage for medical work. With a new car and her physical well being taken care of, she was prepared to turn her life around and start anew.

Before she climbed into bed that night, Bernie set her clock for six. After her visit to Dr. James, she planned to stop at Macy's and pick up the two new suits she had purchased days earlier and left for alterations.

After the alarm clock rang in the morning, she climbed out of bed and dug her gym shorts and running shoes out of the closet. She didn't need to look into the mirror to know it was time to get her body back into shape. A good run would start the day and the new life. Now in her early forties, her body was due for a little tune up.

After a short run, Bernie took a hot shower and then enjoyed a breakfast of coffee, toast and Greek yogurt.

Promptly at eight thirty, she entered the medical clinic on base and was shown into Dr. James' office.

"Thanks for coming in so early," Dr. James said. "I had to change all my appointments around today. Have to take my father to visit a nursing home this afternoon. He can't live alone anymore and needs special care. That damn Alzheimer's you know."

"I understand."

"Thank you. Now, like I said on the phone. You are in good health. I have all your records here; blood pressure, urine tests, medical history, a complete set of x-rays, and a list of the few pills that you take. This should be adequate for your next physician to review. Should you need anything else, you can always contact us. I realize that the recent death of your husband has caused you great stress and probably increased your blood pressure just a little; but, now, maybe you can slow down once again. But, be sure to keep up the regular exercise."

"Yes. I'll try to do both," Bernie answered, feeling very small and vulnerable.

"Have you made any definite plans about your future yet, Mrs. Younger?" Dr. James asked softly, coming to stand only inches away from Bernie.

"Not yet." Bernie lifted her chin a little higher. "Gotta see my son graduate from Military school in about a month and see what his future plans are."

The doctor handed Bernie the large packet with all her records in it. "Well, thanks for coming in so early. And, I hope that you'll keep in touch. I would like to hear how you're doing."

"I'll do that. And thank you for caring." Bernie took the packet and walked out of the clinic. She got in her car and headed toward Macy's Department Store.

"Good morning, Mrs. Younger," the attractive young sales woman said, when she saw Bernie approaching her. "Your two suits have been altered as you wished and are waiting for you in the back. I'll get them for you."

"Thank you." Bernie stood by the counter and waited patiently for the girl to return with the suits.

"I must say that you selected two beautiful suits and with your nice slim figure, you'll wow everyone," the girl said as she brought the bag to the counter. "Your selection of the Chanel gray suit and the cranberry Dior suit are just perfect for you. And I'm certain that you'l be glad that you had them shortened just a bit."

Bernie smiled and gave a little nod. "I did like your suggestion for the length."

As she handed the bag to Bernie, the clerk added, "Oh, Mrs. Younger, since this is the grand opening of our designer clothing department; we have a salon gift certificate for you. It's good for the next six weeks and includes a facial, a manicure and a pedicure."

"Thank you," Bernie replied as she stuffed the certificate into her purse and picked up the garment bag. "I've never had any of those. So it will be a real treat. Now I must get going. My stomach is reminding me that I didn't eat much breakfast."

As she headed for home, Bernie's cell phone rang. She pulled into a strip mall to answer it. "Hello. Hello."

"Is this Mrs. Younger? Grant Younger's mother."

"Yes. This is she. How can I help you?"

"You don't know me, Mrs. Younger. My name is Sandy Rivers."

"Yes?"

"I'm a close friend of your son, Grant. He's in the hospital and he asked me to call you."

Bernie's mouth went dry and heart pounded so hard that she could almost hear it. "He's in the hospital! Why? I just saw him yesterday. What's wrong?"

There was a long pause, before Sandy answered. "After he got back to school he had a severe attack of pain in his abdomen. He was rushed to the hospital, where they did a bunch of tests last night and early this morning. They think that there is something wrong with his kidneys."

A boulder suddenly came to rest upon Bernie's chest. "Where is he?"

"St. Joe's Hospital in Middleton. Could you please come? And hurry." Sandy's voice was barely a whisper.

"I'm on my way. Take care of my son until I get there."

Bernie hung up the phone, turned on the ignition, wheeled the car out of the strip mall and headed for home.

As she pulled into the parking spot outside her apartment, she saw Joy working in her front yard. Bernie jumped out of the car and ran over to her, yelling. "I just got a call from a friend of Grant's. He's in the hospital in Middleton. I'm driving there right now. Please keep an eye on my place while I'm gone. I'll give you a call as soon as I learn anything."

Joy found herself washed in a flood of compassion. What else could happen to her friend? She gave her a quick hug. "Keep me informed."

"I will." She ran into the house, grabbed a large suitcase from the closet and threw undergarments, shoes, jeans, blouses into the bag. She scurried to the bathroom and gathered up her makeup, hair dryer and everyday medications. She tossed them into the bag, changed into a comfortable outfit for traveling and headed out the door.

In the car, she clenched the steering wheel and told herself to calm down as she headed toward the highway. Please Lord, watch over my boy. He's all I've got now.

It would take three and a half hours to reach Middletown and the hospital. And Bernie was thankful for the GPS in her new car that would be great help in finding her way through the town to the hospital.

# Chapter 9

When she arrived at St. Joe's Hospital, Bernie jumped out of her car and handed the keys to the valet parking attendant. She dashed into the building and approached the woman at the reception desk.

A knot was tightening inside Bernie and her blood ran cold—fear growing large enough to consume her. "My son, Grant Younger, was admitted here. Where is he?" she managed to croak.

The elderly volunteer, dressed in a green and white uniform, informed her that he was on the fourth floor and pointed toward the elevators. Without waiting to hear the room number, Bernie raced down the hall.

She shifted nervously from one foot to the other as the elevator seemed to take forever to reach the fourth floor and another eternity for the door to open. She sprang out of the elevator and ran out hurriedly, stopping at the nurses' station.

"Please tell me where my son is," she asked frantically.

"And who are you looking for Madam?" the nurse asked, looking up from her computer.

"My son. My son. His name is..." Bernie paused for a few seconds. She stared at the nurse with panic in her eyes. "I'm so nervous that I can't think straight."

Concerned at Bernie's extreme anxiety, the nurse got up and walked around the nurses' station to her. Taking Bernie's hands in hers she said, "Take a deep breath. Tell me your name." Bernie gave a big sigh and tried to calm herself. "I'm Bernadine Younger and my son, Grant, is supposed to be a patient on this floor."

"Oh yes, Mrs. Younger. I'm Nurse Caldwell. Your son is at the end of the hall. Please follow me. He's in a private room. We're filled to capacity and that was the only room available when he was admitted. Right now, Dr. Patel is with him." She sounded sympathetic and concerned.

Bernie followed the nurse to the end of the hall, where the door to young Grant's room was closed. "Let me check on your son and the doctor," the nurse said.

"Please nurse, can't I go in?" Bernie pleaded.

"Just give me a moment," the nurse replied. Her heart went out to Bernie. She tapped briefly on the door and then entered. Within a few moments, she exited the room with a doctor behind her. "Mrs. Younger, this is Dr. Patel. He's been examining your son."

She turned to the doctor. "And this is Grant's mother, Mrs. Younger."

Dr. Patel was short, but was built with broad shoulders and deep-set assessing brown eyes. He looked like he could run five miles and not break a sweat. He stepped forward and shook Bernie's hand.

"How is my son?" Bernie squeaked. "Now can I see him?"

"In just a few minutes. We need to talk first," Dr. Patel answered cautiously. "There is a private lounge at the end of the hall. Let's go down there and I'll update you on your son's condition."

"But, I want to see him now," Bernie whispered.

"Please Mrs. Younger, follow me. We must talk first."

Because of his insistence, she followed him to the lounge.

After they were both comfortably seated, Dr. Patel leaned forward and lowered his voice. "When your son arrived last night at the emergency room, I was called. He was conscious and in extreme pain in his abdomen. My first concern was to ease his pain. After a short examination I thought that he might have a hernia, a ruptured appendix or a kidney stone. I ordered several tests including blood tests and a CAT scan, trying to determine just what the exact cause of his pain was."

Bernie didn't move. She sat as if frozen to the spot. Frozen, by fear, no doubt. And by uncertainty.

The doctor continued, "When we got the results of the tests

back, my colleague and I carefully went over them together. We determined that Mr. Younger's kidneys were in a state of extreme failure."

Bernie looked stricken. Tears stung her eyes and she blinked against them. "What can you do for him? Can you put him on some medicine or dialysis?"

Trying to soften the blow of what he was about to say, Dr. Patel sighed and answered compassionately, "I'm afraid that future tests this morning have revealed that it is too late for either of these options. Fortunately, my friend, Dr. Knox, from John Hopkins, who is a specialist in this field, is in town for a few days. He went over the tests with me. And we both agreed that your son is one sick boy. He has renal failure and very aggressive cancer in both of his kidneys. Before the cancer spreads outside the kidneys, we need to remove both of them in order to save his life."

Bernie could not believe what she had just heard. She was nearly hysterical with fear. She couldn't think. Her heart was beating so heavily that she could hardly breathe. She whispered, "When do you plan to remove them?"

"At once, I've given Grant morphine through an IV tube and he is resting comfortably. Dr. Knox has agreed to assist me in the operation and we will remove them as soon as possible."

She drew in a deep calming breath. She turned toward him, her expression all business now. "How long can he live without them?"

"Not very long. We need to try to find a transplant for him."

"What about me? I'm his mother. Maybe, I can donate one of my kidneys to him." Her fear was so great that she thought it would consume her.

"That would be ideal, if it's possible. Living donors genetically related are the best possible candidates. That way your son would need less immunosuppressive therapy afterwards to ward off rejection of the new kidney. If you like we can immediately schedule you for tests to see if you can be a donor."

"I would like that," Bernie responded. "I'm only forty-three years old and in good shape. I just had a complete physical. In fact, I have all my medical records with me, including X-rays. I just picked them up from the doctor's office earlier today."

"Good. The kidney is the easiest organ to transplant and tissue typing is simple. The organ is easy to remove and implant and live donors can be used without difficulty. If individuals with chronic renal failure have a living donor available, he or she may undergo pre-emptive transplantation before dialysis is needed. In most cases, the barely functioning existing kidneys are not removed, but in your son's case this would not be the ideal situation. We need to remove the cancerous kidneys."

Bernie made a choked sound of anguish. "If Grant gets the kidney transplant will he be okay?"

"The twenty-four hours following the operation will determine if it's successful. Because you are a relative, his chances of rejection are much less. Ideally, a kidney transplant should take place before a patient begins dialysis. Some kidney transplant recipients have lived for thirty or forty years afterwards and science is improving every day. So your son could probably live to a ripe old age with your kidney." Genuinely touched by Bernie's attitude, he added, "And if I know you, my fine courageous lady, you will always be at his side."

"Now, can I see my son?" she asked, trying to sound cavalier about it and not as frightened as she actually was.

"Yes. Of course. But, I must tell you he is still in some discomfort."

Upon seeing his mother and the doctor enter the room, Grant struggled to get himself into a sitting position, his face twisting in an awful grimace of pain.

After mother and son had a long serious talk about his condition, Bernie told him that she planned to donate one of her kidneys to him.

At first Grant reacted angrily to this, but, the doctor assured him that his mother would probably recover quickly and not suffer any long term effects. She could easily live a long and healthy life with only one kidney.

Bernie and Dr. Patel left the room after their visit with Grant and walked downstairs to the main floor of the hospital, where Dr.

Patel immediately arranged for Bernie to have the necessary tests to make sure that her tissue was compatible with Grant's and that the transferred kidney would be readily accepted by Grant's body.

Before the doctor could leave, Bernie ran to the car and got the packet of her medical records and X-rays. She brought them in to him.

"Since you just had all this blood work and tests done, it will save us a lot of time today, Mrs. Younger," he said. "I will have the lab compare your tissue samples with that of your son. If they are compatible, we will schedule the transplant for early tomorrow morning."

Dr. Patel looked briefly through the packet that Bernie had given him. "Oh, by the way, Mrs. Younger, I didn't realize that you were Major Grant Younger's wife. I mean his widow. You have my sincere condolences at the loss of your husband. I served with him briefly overseas and found him to be a most honorable man."

Bernie looked at him with sadness in her eyes. Normally, Bernie would have a whole string of good remarks on her tongue. She always had comebacks ready before they were needed, but now everything was frozen. She couldn't say a word. She knew that the rest of the world, including her son, were not aware of Grant's many faults and she intended to keep it that way. And, right now, it was her son who was most important.

"I believe that the army will take care of the expense of your son's operation and the transfer of your kidney if it is compatible. After you have your tests, you can wait in your son's room for us. Dr. Knox and I will look over the results of the tests and meet with you there."

Bernie was ushered into one of the nearby departments, where her tissue sample was taken. Then, she went up to Grant's room to sit and wait for the results.

She was sitting in a chair next to Grant's bed, when after nearly an hour the doctors knocked on the door and entered the room.

Dr. Patel introduced Bernie to Dr. Knox. Then, turning to Dr. Knox, Dr. Patel added, "Mrs. Younger is the recent widow of Major Grant Younger. I served with him briefly in Iraq and he was a true soldier."

Dr. Knox offered his condolences to Bernie, then added, "Now, for some good news. Your tissue is compatible with your son's and we will remove both of his kidneys. We have scheduled two operating rooms for tomorrow morning at seven. While we are working on Grant, another team of doctors will remove one of your kidneys. For a lady in her early forties, you appear to be in extremely good health and we expect you to have a rapid recovery from the surgery." The fierceness in his eyes told her that this was a serious situation.

"How do you perform the operations and how long does it take?" Bernie asked.

"We will use the De Vinci system for both you and Grant. It is a robot-assisted technology that is remarkable. It's an advanced form of laparoscopic surgery that allows us to do precision work with less trauma to the patient. We no longer have to have a large incision for either of you. A laparoscopic camera and robotic probes are inserted through four half-inch incisions. We use hand controls and foot pedals to manipulate the robotic arms. The probes translate the surgeon's hand movements and adjust themselves to compensate for the natural tremor of the human hand. The equipment is set to make the tiniest movements with rock steady precision," Dr. Patel said.

"The patient is safe, the operation minimally invasive and the recovery time is shorter. The twelve hours after surgery will be most critical. We will admit you to the hospital right now, if that is okay with you. And be sure not to eat after midnight. You can probably both leave the hospital in two or three days. Of course, we ask you both to stay nearby for several weeks for follow up," Dr. Knox added. In his eyes, Bernie saw real compassion. He was used to dealing with his patient's apprehensions.

Bernie folded her hands in front of her, but the doctors noticed that they trembled. "Thank you, Doctor."

The next morning, after her surgery, Bernie found herself returning to consciousness in the recovery room.

"Mrs. Younger, nice to see you with your eyes open. I'm Nurse Karen and I will be taking care of you while you are in recovery. I'm told that your surgery went very well."

Bernie ran her tongue around her mouth to moisten it before she asked, "And how is my son?"

"He's in the other recovery room and resting very comfortably. All went well with his surgery also. Dr. Patel will be in to see you later and will give you an update. Soon, I'll get an orderly to take you up to your room. Once you're up there, you can check with the nurse to see if the doctor has ordered a light breakfast for you. If you feel well enough later, you can probably go to your son's room and visit with him."

After Bernie was settled in her room the nurse said, "You have a couple of visitors—the parking attendant and a Ms. Rivers."

# Chapter 10

"Please tell them to come in," Bernie answered.

The door opened slowly and a red haired young man with freckles sprinkled across his face entered the room. "Good morning, Mrs. Younger, I'm Tommy, the hospital parking valet. I noticed that you left your large suitcase in the back of your car and I thought that you might need it since it appeared that you stayed overnight."

"Thank you," Bernie responded. "I guess that I was so busy getting my records, that I didn't even think of my suitcase. How did you know it was mine?"

He heard the confusion in her voice. "Oh, the other kid that worked with me told me your name. I found out at the desk what room you were in. When I got up to this floor, I heard about you and your son, the future West Point cadet." His face broke out in a big grin. "I hope to be in the army after I graduate from high school."

"Well, I'm certain that you'll make a fine soldier. Thank you, once again for your kindness and let me give you something for your time."

"Oh, no. But I would like to visit with your son while he's here."

She shrugged her shoulders, unsure if Grant would feel like having visitors. "Today is probably not too good for him. Why don't you stop by tomorrow?"

"I think I'll do that. And you're one courageous lady to donate your kidney to your son," the young man, said with some embarrassment.

After he left the room, a tiny young lady with short curly black hair entered. "Mrs. Younger, I'm Sandy Rivers, Grant's friend. I'm the one who called you the other day about Grant."

Bernie looked up at this petite young woman and thought

immediately that she reminded her of a movie star. Sandy appeared to be only about five feet tall with eyes that were a piercingly deep shade of green. Her complexion was flawless and she had a delicate pink rosebud mouth. Bernie decided that Sandy was one of the most exquisite girls that she had ever seen. Wow. Grant really has good taste in the ladies, she thought to herself.

"Yes. Sandy, thank you so much for calling me. I got here as soon as I could."

Bernie extended her hands out to the girl, who walked over and took them in hers. "It was so nice of you to be so concerned about my son," Bernie said with a small smile curving her lips. "Sit down next to my bed. I need to get to know you better."

As they talked, Bernie was surprised to hear that Grant had told his father about his relationship with Sandy. "Yes, Major Younger even called me one time and talked to me about our dating," Sandy said, hesitantly. "He told me to go slowly with Grant, because he had his future planned for him. And, apparently, Grant's future was with West Point and I should be sure that I wanted to be involved with a military man."

Bernie's head drooped briefly, and then she squared her shoulders and tilted her chin. "And what did you reply to that?" she asked.

"I simply told him that I understood and we would take things slowly," Sandy answered. "I only talked to the Major that one time. But, I'm surprised to hear that neither Grant nor his father mentioned me to you."

"Yes, so am I," Bernie replied sadly. It took every ounce of determination to keep her voice level. "But the two were always very close."

Sandy continued slowly, as if she was weighing what she was about to say. "I'm extremely concerned about Grant. We've been dating for several months," she paused, and with a deep breath said, "I love him very much."

"Did you go in to see him before you came to see me? How is he doing?" Bernie's voice was filled with anxiety.

"Yes. I was sorry I couldn't be here for him the last few days. But,

I had exams at school." Her expression was one of grave unease, as she continued, "He's sleeping now, but the nurse said he was doing well. She also said that she could take you in a wheelchair later to visit Grant. I hope I can join you. I'd like to spend the rest of the day with him."

From the expression in Sandy' eyes, Bernie could see that she cared deeply for Grant and had no intention of leaving his side now that she had finally gotten here. "That would be lovely and I welcome the opportunity to get to know you better. Tell me more about yourself and Grant and how the two of you met."

As Sandy talked on and on about Grant, Bernie could easily see why her son could have become enchanted with this beautiful young woman.

Later, the nurse came to Bernie's room and announced that Grant was now awake and settled in his room and that the ladies could visit him. She helped Bernie get into a wheel chair.

With the nurse leading the way, Sandy pushed Bernie down the hall to Grant's room. She pushed the wheelchair right up against Grant's bed and Bernie leaned over to give her son a hug. The love in Bernie's eyes was reflected in that of her son's as he kissed his mother.

Grant glanced up at Sandy, who with tears running down her face, was standing beside the wheelchair. He motioned for her to come forward. Sandy rushed to him, leaned over, embraced him and gave him a big kiss.

He was all choked up as he looked up to his mother. Then forcing a smile onto his face and brightness into his voice, he said, "Look at all of us crying like babies. And, you look great, Mom. How are you feeling?"

Bernie's hands started to tremble. She steadied them by folding them in her lap. "I'm feeling good. And you?"

A solid lump formed in Grant's throat at the thought of the great gift that his mother had just given him—a new life. After several deep breaths, he felt ready to face the future. He straightened his shoulders and put a firm smile on his face. "I'm getting stronger by the minute. The kidney is working fine so far. And I'm part of you now, Mom."

"Son, you've been a part of me, all our lives," Bernie replied, with tears streaming down her cheeks.

The nurse entered the room and pulled a rolling table in front of Bernie. "Here's your lunch, Mrs. Younger. And I have a tray for your son too. We want both of you to eat something light today. Tomorrow, you should both be able to resume your normal diets."

As he started to drink his broth, Grant looked over at Sandy and then at his mother. "I hope that you've had the chance to get acquainted with my girlfriend, Mom."

Bernie looked up, startled. She had never heard Grant mention this lovely young creature before and now she was surprised to hear him refer to her as his girlfriend.

Grant noticed the question in his mother's eyes. "Sandy and I've been dating for awhile. She was sorry she couldn't make it to Dad's funeral. She had exams."

Sandy swept her hair away from her face and sucked in a deep breath. "Yes. I tried to get out of them. But they couldn't reschedule them for another time."

"And how did you do on the tests?" Bernie asked, as she sipped her broth.

"I think I did extremely well. At least, I hope so."

Then, as Grant and Bernie continued their conversation, Sandy looked at them with a quiet contemplation. She could not help but feel what a wonderful mother and son these two were. In the back of her mind, she hoped that she would someday be part of their family.

After both of the patients finished their lunches, Bernie pushed her table away. "Now, Son," she said casually, "Tell me how you're really feeling."

Grant could see the deep concern in his mother's expression. "Well, Dr. Patel told me all went well with the transplant and maybe, in a few days, I can head back to school. And what about you, Mom? How are you doing?"

Bernie sat upright in her wheelchair. It was more than her body mending, it was her spirit. "My surgery went well and I think that maybe I can leave the hospital tomorrow. But you're not going to live at school when you get out of here. I'm going to rent an apartment in Middleton and you're staying with me while you recover from the surgery or until you finish school. I want you to just relax and get stronger in the next few weeks. That's my orders."

"Okay, Mom. You're the boss for now. But, I have more news to tell you. It's about my future. My former roommate invited me to come to California and live with him near Santa Barbara after I graduate. I spent a week with him last year and it's beautiful there. I was offered a job in his dad's office and I could continue my schooling there."

"So, that's your plan then," Bernie asked cautiously. A cold feeling started at the top of her head and moved downward until she felt chilled. She did not want Grant to leave her just yet.

Grant looked over at Sandy and smiled as he continued, "Well, no. I turned the job down. I decided that after graduation next month, I'm going to follow in Dad's footsteps and attend West Point. Colonel Edwards is sending me the application and he's going to sponsor me. He had Dad as a cadet many years ago and said that with my good grades and his sponsorship I should have no trouble getting in."

Bernie realized that the past few days had brought strength and maturity to her son and that he was now ready to plan his own future. "Wow! That's some plan, Grant."

"You believe it's the right decision for me, then?"

"Yes. I definitely think that you should go for it and your father would be very proud of you. But from now on, only good memories for the three of us."

The three exchanged big grins. For the next few moments, none spoke as each pondered the future.

Finally, calm settled over Bernie. "Hang onto your hat, Grant Younger IV, your announcement has helped me to make a big decision about myself. My dear friend, April, contacted me a few days ago to tell me that the bank that I worked at before I was married was bought out. April is the district manager of a big new

First Federal that's opening in about a month. April offered me a job as assistant manager."

"Wow! That's terrific Mom," Grant said.

"That's one reason why I was planning on taking an apartment in Middleton. Now, that you're planning to go to West Point, I'll call her and tell her 'yes' on the job. This way we can stay close to each other too."

"That sounds like a great plan, Mrs. Younger," Sandy said.

Grant leaned forward. "I love it that you're taking charge of your own life once again, Mom. And Sandy is hoping to work at Middleton Hospital after she gets her nursing degree."

"I'm planning to do something very bold when I leave this hospital," Bernie added. "I've going to make a date with Macy's. They owe me a complete makeover. And Grant, I hope that you'll hang on to this girl."

He looked up at the two of them and grinned. "That's my goal, Mom."

Sandy moved closer to the bed and with shaking hands took Grant's in hers. "I really hope that I'll be included in yours and your mother's future."

He kissed her fingers. "I'm counting on it." He picked up a bottle of water from his hospital tray. "I toast to our future together—the three Amigos."

Looking at Bernie, Sandy raised her hand in salute. "Gosh, Mrs. Younger, you must love this son of yours very much. Giving up one of your kidneys was really something. You are truly one courageous woman."

Bernie eyes reflected her happiness. "When you really love someone, Sandy, nothing is impossible—even miracles."

"Yes. And you're still a young and attractive woman, Mom. Sandy says that her folks have an Orkin man who is single and very handsome," Grant said with a big chuckle.

Sandy nodded. "Yes. He is really cute in his uniform."

"Uniform?" Bernie thought for a few moments. Then, with a deep sigh, shook her head firmly. "No more uniforms for me."

# Getting Her Life Back
## Chapter 1

"Hear yea. Hear yea. All Rise. Night Court is in session. The Honorable Judge Harold Gomes, presiding," the clerk at the Night Court in Upper Manhattan, New York, called out. "Please be seated."

The bailiff, Charlie Strong, riffled though his papers and realized only three cases were on the docket at the present time. The first case was Juan Rodriguez, who was arrested for being drunk and disorderly.

Charlie knew that two things would be happening soon to change his personal circumstances. Judge Gomes, who was approaching the age of sixty-five, would soon be retiring. He was a tall, stout man with eyes that burrowed deep under his bushy eyebrows, and whiskey–colored hair with shots of gray at the temples. When it was discovered he had extremely high blood pressure, the judge's health suddenly became his top priority. His doctors suggested he take daily medicine and slow down. Because all his retirement benefits were very good, Judge Gomes decided to retire early. And wanting to avoid the cold New York weather, he planned to move to the land of sunshine—and he didn't mean Arizona.

Having lost his wife to cancer the previous year, he was now setting his sights on retiring to Florida. His sister and her husband lived in a mobile home park in Clearwater which was filled with retirees from New York and, when he learned that the double wide-home, located next to them, was for sale, he had her put a down payment on it.

The second thing that would directly affect Charlie's life was the fact that a decision had recently been made by the city council to tear down the old court house and erect a new one across the street in the next two or three years. The city was in the process of accepting bids for the design and the construction.

The judge was not the only one in the court room contemplating retiring. Tall and lean with thinning gray hair, sixty-year-old Charlie had put in enough years with the city that he could also take an early retirement. So when the judge left, Charlie thought he might retire, but would continue to live in New York City with his wife and their two cats. "Can't leave my New York Yankees," he told his wife.

He was considering taking his pension early from the city. He knew he could work for his cousin in his small bistro on weekends to make extra cash. He realized even though he only weighted one hundred and sixty pounds, he was on his feet all day and in a couple of years his weak knees would start to give out and he would probably need to have an operation on them. He and his wife, who were a good team, had been putting money in CD's and IRA's for years. He would now have the time to work extensively on his leaded glass work in his small garage. And yes, he and his wife might even travel some. However, they definitely wouldn't give up their volunteer work, taking meals to the homeless.

Standing in front of Judge Gomes, was the short, stout and broad shouldered Juan Rodriguez. The paper in front of the judge indicated that he was thirty-one and unemployed.

The judge looked down from the bench at Juan and with zero warmth in his smile asked, "How do you plea, Mr. Rodriguez?"

Rodriguez hung his head and said nothing.

After a lengthy pause, the judge called out, "Your plea, Sir. Guilty or not guilty are the choices."

Juan hesitated and rubbed his chin, then replied quietly, "Guilty, your Honor."

The judge slammed his gavel down. His gruff voice rumbled, "Sorry, this is your third strike and you're out. Three days in the county jail and you must attend AA meetings for six months."

Juan released his breath in a gusty sigh. Then muttering to himself in Spanish, he added, "Maybe this will finally help me to fight the demon."

Charlie motioned for the officer to escort Juan out of the court room and to a holding cell, pending his transfer to the county jail.

Charlie looked down at his docket and announced, "Next case, your Honor, is William Thomas, better known as Willie Thomas. He was arrested for eating his supper at Chung Lee's Chinese Restaurant and skipping out without paying his bill. He was running down the street, a block away from the restaurant, when the arresting office caught up with him. He did not resist arrest."

The judge looked down at Willie. "How do you plea, Mr. Thomas?"

The elderly black man with curly white hair, wearing a dirty sweat shirt and jeans, glanced down at his worn sneakers, then looked up with tears in his eyes. "Guilty, Sir. But this is the first time I've ever been arrested. I lost my job and I was hungry, your Honor. And, I made a dumb mistake."

The judge looked down at him, with sympathy in his eyes, debating how to handle this case. "I guess that I'll have to sentence you to the county jail for seven days. We cannot allow this kind of behavior to happen without consequence."

Just then, someone in the back of the room stood up. "Your Honor, I am Ming Kia, the owner of the restaurant where this man ate. If he would be willing to wash dishes for a week, I will not press charges. My part-time dishwasher quit."

The judge asked Mr. Thomas, "Well, Sir, how you feel about that offer?"

The man stared in amazement at Mr. Kia. Then lifted his head and replied humbly, "I'll do it your Honor." He looked back at Ming Kia. "And thank you."

The judge slammed his gavel down. "Charges dismissed. He's all yours Mr. Kia."

As Charlie led Willie to Mr. Kia, he said, "This is your good deed for the day and I hope that it works out well for you. "

"I hope so too," Mr. Kia responded.

The city streets of Manhattan were gradually changing for the better, now that the newly elected mayor had taken office. The number of crimes committed in the city was down; the X-rated book stores had been closed and the prostitutes had moved from the metropolitan center to the suburbs of the city.

"I'm going to make the streets of New York safe for the people who live here," the mayor had promised prior to his election and he had kept his promise. Tourism was once again flourishing. The restaurant and theater owners were delighted to have welcomed the tourists back. Times Square was now buzzing with activity.

Maybe, because it was Holy Week, and this was Good Friday, only three cases were on the docket at the night court.

"Now, your Honor, one last case," the bailiff announced.

The judge looked at his watch. "Let's see one more case," he said, "and my wife and I can attend Good Friday services at St. Patrick's."

"The State of New York now calls the case of Frances Taylor. Ms. Taylor is charged with causing a disturbance and resisting arrest," the bailiff said as a young woman sitting on a nearby bench stood up.

Getting anxious to wrap up this court session, the judge looked quickly at the papers in front of him and asked, "How do you plea, Mr. Taylor?"

"That's Frances, with an "E" your honor. I'm a female."

Startled, the judge put his glasses on, stared again at his paperwork. He peered down at the young woman who looked to be in her mid twenties. He noticed that underneath the dirt, she had a lovely peaches and cream complexion and striking blue eyes. She stood about five feet four and had a cloud of blond hair that now looked as if it had been whipped by the rotor blades of a helicopter. He could visualize that with her dirty hair shampooed and combed, her face washed and clean clothing, she would look very attractive.

He sucked in his breath and cleared his throat. "Yes. So you are. I'm sorry. Well, Frances with an 'E' how do you plea?"

"Not guilty, your Honor, on all counts," she answered despairingly.

Still looking at his paperwork, the judge added, "Well, I see that you have no criminal record prior to this."

"Yes sir. And may I make a statement?"

He narrowed his eyes, all traces of patience gone. "Hurry up. You're the last case and I'm anxious to get out of here."

Frances drew herself up to her full height, barely holding her anger in check. "Well, first of all, Sir, I was screaming loudly because the police officer was hurting me. I was in the alley behind Judson's bar, going through the dumpster, looking for food. Two men, who appeared to be homeless, were sitting on the ground beside the dumpster. An officer came along. He apparently thought that I was with them and tried to arrest the three of us for vagrancy or something. When, I resisted arrest, the officer grabbed me by the arms and tried to cuff me. I tried to fight him off, telling him that I was just looking for food. He wouldn't listen to me. I started screaming because of the way he yanked on my arms and called me names. At no time did I cause a disturbance nor did I resist arrest—I merely protested and he shouldn't have roughed me up."

The bailiff stepped forward. "Sir, that was Officer Mitchell. This is the third time this week, that we've had such a complaint against him."

The judge looked thoughtfully at Frances as she continued, "Anyway, your Honor, I hadn't eaten since yesterday, so I was just looking for food."

"In a dumpster?" he admonished with a frown.

"Yes." Then she added crisply, working to mask the edge of shame in her voice, "Sometimes I get lucky and find fresh sandwiches that the bar throws away."

"How old are you, Ms. Taylor?" The judge noticed that Frances's hands were clenched into fists at her side.

"I'm twenty-four," she replied sharply.

"And where do you live?"

Frances took in a great shuddering breath. She hiked her chin up. Angry color strained her cheeks. "Right now, I'm out on the street. I used to live with my grandmother, but she went to a nursing home and passed away after a few months."

The Judge heaved a big sigh and thought for a few moments. "It looks as though you've gone about as low as you can go. What schooling do you have?"

"Well. I did graduate from architectural school. Right now, I would do anything—clean houses, scrub floors, whatever. Once I get some money, I know I can turn my life around."

A small sound of fright passed her lips. "But, please judge, don't put me in jail."

A feeling of dread coiled in Frances's stomach. She wondered whether things would ever be right again.

Judge Gomes had heard this story many times in his twenty years of service on the bench and he was inclined to be somewhat tough with the people who appeared before him. But, somehow, he felt a strong twinge of sympathy for this proud young woman.

Charlie stepped up to the bench and whispered in the judge's ear. The judge looked at him. "You're sure?"

"Yes, your Honor. I talked to the head maintenance man earlier."

The judge motioned for him to step back. Then looked down at Frances and smiled. "This may or may not be your lucky day or shall we say, night, Ms. Taylor. The bailiff has just informed me that the scrub lady for the court house has quit. In fact, they need someone, immediately to replace her. Would you be interested in the job?"

Frances's head snapped up. "Yes, Sir. I told you I would do anything to get back on my feet."

"Well, then, I'll set your arrest aside for now and put you in the hands of Mr. Strong. And, if, after a month, you seem to be on the path of straightening out your life, I'll drop all charges against you."

Frances made a sound of disbelief. Her heart began to thunder and her eyes were filled with tears. "Thank you," she replied gratefully. "You won't regret helping me. I promise you, Judge."

"Okay young lady, now go with Charlie." Turning to the bailiff, he added, "She's all yours now, Charlie, and good luck. I'm off to Good Friday services." He pounded the gavel. "Night Court is closed."

# Chapter 2

The bailiff took Frances by the arm and escorted her out of the courtroom. "I'm Charlie Strong. Please have a seat right here." He guided her over to a hard wooden bench in the hallway. "I'll check with the maintenance supervisor about that job. But I hope you realize it's not very glamorous with night hours and very hard work."

Frances sat down gingerly, looked up at him and replied with apparent worry in her voice, "Please Mr. Strong. I need that job. You heard what the judge said. I need to get my life turned around."

Her simple words ate at his heart. "Okay. I'll be right back. First, I have to turn out the lights in the courtroom. But, don't fret. There's still light in the hall and I won't put you in the dark."

Charlie left Frances and headed for the maintenance office on the third floor. About fifteen minutes later he approached Frances once again and sat down beside her. "Well, you're one lucky young lady. When, I told Eddie Purdue, maintenance supervisor, about your dire situation, he agreed to give you a chance."

Frances gave a sigh of relief as he continued, "He said you can start tonight at eleven. You'll have a two-day trial and if you do good work over the weekend, he said he would put you on full time on Monday."

Frances raised herself higher on the bench. Her world was turning right side up once again. With shy hesitation in her voice, she smiled and asked, "Any chance you might know how much I'll get paid?"

"I would guess about ten dollars an hour. But I do need to warn you that your boss, Eddie, is a tough task master. He'll make sure that you earn your money."

Frances's smile deepened. "I'm not afraid of hard work. And I appreciate the chance. You're an angel."

"Tomorrow morning at seven, you may not think so." Charlie stood up and took her by the hand. "Now, you're coming home with me. No questions asked." He tugged on her arm. "I want you to stay with my wife and me until you get back on your feet."

Frances secured her arm resolutely through his. "You're sure about this? Won't your wife object to you bringing a stranger home?"

"Well, this is a first." He grinned at the irony. "But, you appear to be a nice person who needs a little help. And my wife is a very special lady when it comes to helping people."

Frances blushed a delicate shade of pink and stammered, "Well, then, thank you. I'll accept your help because I need it so desperately. But, I'll pay you back as soon as I can. Honest."

"Don't worry about it." He fixed her with a steady gaze. "I don't have a car so we'll have to walk to my house. It's raining, but I found an extra umbrella in the lost and found for you. I only live a few blocks from here. Let's hurry so you have time for a bite of supper. You need to get back here by ten-thirty in order to start on time." Grinning broadly, he added, "You don't want to be late for your first night of work."


With his key, Charlie opened the front door to an old brownstone apartment building just three blocks from the courthouse. "Follow me," he said as he led Frances upstairs to his two bedroom, two bath apartment.

Unlocking the door to the apartment, he added, "This place is just the right size for the wife and me. My brother-in-law rents to us really cheap. He owns a couple of these brownstones and does quite well. Even spends the winters in Miami."

As they stepped inside the doorway, Charlie yelled out, "Marge, I'm home. And I brought someone for supper."

Wiping her hands on a dish towel, a short heavyset gray-haired woman rushed out of the kitchen. Stopping abruptly in the doorway to the living room, she took a long look at Frances, who was dirty and disheveled and dressed in filthy clothes.

"This is Frances Taylor," Charlie said as he walked over to his wife, leaned down and gave her a quick kiss. "And she could use a good meal and a hot shower before she starts work at the courthouse tonight at eleven."

Quickly composing herself, Marge smiled, strolled over to Frances and grabbed her hands in hers. "I'm so glad to meet you. Hope you like beef stew and homemade bread, because that's what we're having tonight."

"Oh, I love beef stew. And I can smell the bread already. It smells wonderful," Frances said, a bright smile lighting her face.

Charlie put his arm around his wife's waist. Fixing a firm look upon his face, he added, "And, I told Frances that she is welcome to stay in our spare room for as long as she needs."

Not hesitating for a second, Marge smiled and nodded, then took Frances by the hand. "Come with me. I'll show you to your room and you can take a hot shower while Charlie helps me set the table for supper. Any luggage Dear?"

Frances shrugged her shoulders and answered shyly, "No."

"That's okay. I think I have everything that you might need," Marge replied.

Frances could not believe how kind and receptive this woman was to a complete stranger.

Marge led Frances down the hall to the guest bedroom, led her inside and opened the door to the adjoining bathroom. "You'll find towels in the closet and there's combs and makeup in the drawer under the counter. I'll lay out some clean underwear and a pair of jeans and a shirt on the bed for you."

Frances was speechless. She could not believe the generosity of this couple she had just met.

"Once, you're showered and dressed, come out to the kitchen. I'll have supper ready."

"Thank you, Mrs. Strong. You and your husband have been so

kind," Frances replied, tears filling her eyes.

"You must call me Marge. And we want you to stay with us for as long as necessary for you to get back on your feet. God has been so good to Charlie and me, helping others once in a while is the least that we can do in return for His kindness."

Frances gave Marge a brief hug. "I can't thank you and your husband enough for your goodness. And by the way, who do I thank for the clothes and toiletries?"

"They belonged to Charlie's sister. She passed away not long ago." She stared at Frances. "In fact, not only are you about the same size as her, you even look like her and have some of her mannerisms."

As Marge left the bedroom, Frances could not help but wonder if her resemblance to his deceased sister had motivated Charlie to decide to help her. Shrugging her shoulders and thankful for her good luck, Frances stripped down and stepped into the hot shower. As she shampooed her hair, she thought about how good it felt to be clean again.

After the shower, she put on the clean clothes, combed her hair and applied some blush and lipstick to her face. As she walked into the kitchen, Marge looked over at her. She had not realized how beautiful Frances was. "My goodness, you really look like Charlie's sister."

"Thank you. I certainly feel like a new woman."

"Sometime I'll tell you all about her," Marge whispered as Charlie entered the kitchen.

After the delicious hot supper, Charlie handed Frances two keys. "Here are the keys for both the front door to the building and to our apartment. This way, you can let yourself in when you come home from work."

Frances took them from his hand and placed them in the pocket of the jeans. She still could not believe how trusting these people were.

"And be sure to grab a light jacket and one of the umbrellas by the front door, in case you need them," Marge added.

At ten fifteen, Frances headed out of the front door of the

apartment building, rounded the corner and walked down the dimly lighted street toward the courthouse.

Turning her face up into the gentle rain that was falling, Frances decided not to put up the umbrella. The jacket was sufficient to protect her clothes and the gentle mist helped to erase the past sorrows from her soul.

As per Charlie's earlier instructions, she walked up to the side entrance to the courthouse and rang the buzzer. A few minutes later, the door opened and a tall skinny black man with frizzy black hair, slightly graying at the temples, stood in the doorway.

"Hi, there. You must be Frances Taylor, Charlie's friend. I'm Eddie Purdue, the maintenance supervisor. I knew Charlie would see that you got here on time. Come on in and follow me." He stepped back and allowed Frances to enter the building.

"Thank you. I'm glad to meet you." Frances extended her hand to him.

He shook it vigorously and looked her up and down. "You're kind'a small to be scrubbing floors."

Frances's face sobered. "Yes, but, I'm not afraid to work."

"Let's hop on the service elevator. This building has three floors and I'd like you to start on the first floor and work your way up, cleaning the floors and rest rooms."

When they arrived on the third floor, Eddie led the way to a large cleaning supply room. "My office is next door, this is where we keep the cleaning supplies. Here's a zippered jump suit and a pair of boots you can wear. Also take a couple of pairs of rubber gloves."

He showed Frances how to operate the cleaning and buffing machines. "Sometimes you have to get down on your hands and knees and pre-treat a bad spot before you can run the machine. Here's a hand scrubber you can use on bad gum spots. Tonight, I'd like you to just clean and buff the first floor." He stared down at her intently. "Think you can handle it?"

Frances said firmly, "Yes. Sir. I can do it. I won't let you down."

"You can clean the front hall tonight and wax and buff it after a good scrubbing. The first floor takes the most beating from traffic.

Your hours tonight are from eleven to seven in the morning. I'll see you at seven in the morning. You'll work a half day on Saturday, six to ten p.m. Then take Sunday off. It's Easter you know. The place will be locked up tight until Monday morning."

He reached into his pocket and pulled out a card and a sheet of paper. "There's no time clock to punch, just fill out this card with your times. Take a fifteen minute break whenever you want, but, I suggest that you fill out this job application then."

Frances nodded, hoping  she could remember all of Eddie's instructions as he continued, "We don't have a security guard here tonight, so you'll be all alone. Sure you can handle it?"

"Yes." She dug in her heels and answered confidently, "Yes. In fact, I'm anxious to get started."

Reaching into the pocket of his shirt, Eddie pulled out a pen and a tiny scrap of paper. "Here's my phone number, call me if you have any problems."

After Eddie left, Frances was ready to start work on the first floor. She filled a bucket with strong detergent and hot water. Grabbing her scrapping tool, she loaded them onto the cleaning cart. Then pushed the cart and the scrubber and buffing machines into the service elevator, closed the door and descended to the main floor.

As she exited the elevator, she noticed a clock on the wall. She hoped that she had enough time to complete her assigned tasks.

It took almost two hours to scrape the gum off the floor of the main entrance and to scrub it. With hours to go until her quitting time, Frances left the entrance hall to dry while she checked out the restrooms on the main floor. She found them extremely dirty and had to attack the bowls with a cleanser and then use the floor scrubber to wash the floors.

Now, for waxing the main floor, she thought. She applied the wax and waited for it to dry before she attacked it with the large buffing machine. At first the huge and powerful machine started to drag her across the floor, but she soon got control of it. Within a short time, she was working the machine like a pro. When she was finished, she stood back and surveyed her work. She was proud of how well the floor had turned out.

It was shortly before her quitting time when Frances took a tour of the restrooms she had cleaned to size up her work. They were immaculate.

With a sigh of satisfaction for a job well done, she loaded her equipment on the elevator and headed to the third floor maintenance storage room. She put the cleaning supplies away, took off her boots and jumper.

It was time to leave, but there was no sign of Eddie Purdue. She checked his office door. It was locked so she slipped her job application form under the door. Most likely, I'll see Eddie sometime later, she thought.

She slipped into the elevator and headed downstairs. As she walked down the entrance hall to leave, she looked down at the floor, her arms and shoulders aching from the long night's work. "You should like this work, Mr. Purdue. At least, I hope so."

Making sure that the side door to the building locked securely behind her, Frances exited the courthouse and headed to her room in Marge and Charlie's apartment. She quietly crept inside. As she passed the kitchen, she noticed that Marge had left out a box of cereal on the table. Next to it was a note informing Frances that the milk for the cereal was in the refrigerator. The note also indicated that a bag in the refrigerator contained a tuna fish sandwich and a soda. On the nearby counter was a small bag of potato chips and a candy bar. God, what nice people!

Exhausted, Frances crept into the spare bedroom and set the clock for four in the afternoon and then fell into a deep but restful slumber.

After the alarm abruptly interrupted her sound sleep, Frances jumped out of bed, anxious to start the new day and her new life. After a quick hot shower, she dressed, headed to the kitchen and grabbed her snack. There was a small note on the kitchen table from Marge which said they had gone shopping.

Hope I can get used to these crazy working hours, Frances thought as she once again headed for the courthouse.

When she arrived at the side door, the security guard let her in. "You're the new cleaning lady, right?" he asked. He was a round man who appeared to be in his sixties, seventy looming.

"Yes. Frances Taylor," she said.

"Glad to meet you Frances. I'm Harry Willis. You did the entrance floor, Miss?"

"Yes. And?"

"Hell, I can even read the insignia on the floor now. Eddie Purdue will really like your work."

"Thanks. Gotta run. Don't want to be late." Frances headed down the hall.

Frances was humming to herself as she took the elevator up to the third floor once again. I never thought that working would make me feel so good, she thought as she got her equipment and headed for the second floor.

She put on all the lights on the second floor. "Now it's magic time," she said. Standing back and looking down at her task, she decided the old hardwood floors would be even tougher to clean.

"You did great, girl," she whispered to herself when she finally finished them.

Suddenly, she heard a voice call out, "Saw the first floor. Looking good, Ms. Taylor."

She looked up and saw Eddie Purdue standing near the elevators. She wiped her hands on her jumper and walked toward him.

"So far Frances, I'm more than pleased with your work. Stop now for a moment, I want to talk with you."

Frances smiled. "Thank you, Mr. Purdue. I still have to finish up on this floor."

"Well, first come to my office," Eddie said. "Join me in a cup of coffee."

Frances followed him upstairs where he waved her into a chair. "Please call me Eddie and I'll call you Frances if that's okay?"

Frances nodded.

"Well, you appear to have done a fine job. I inspected the first floor and its restrooms. I can't believe you haven't been doing this for years. You're hired permanently. I want you to be here early on Monday morning and plan to start full time. You'll work Mondays and Tuesdays, have Wednesdays off and then work Thursdays and Fridays. Your regular hours will be seven in the morning to three in the afternoon."

"Thank you," Frances whispered.

"Your pay will be ten fifty an hour; but, in three months, you get a raise to fifteen and start full time benefits with dental and health care. Any questions?"

She tipped her head to the side, overcome with gratitude at what she had just heard, "No, Sir. I mean Eddie. And I'll appreciate the benefits and raise later."

He reached in a drawer of his desk, and pulled out a paper. "You'll need to fill out this form for IRS. Glad to have you on board."

"Thank you. I'm very glad for the opportunity."

"You're welcome. See you on Monday and enjoy your Easter Sunday."

Frances rose slowly to her feet. "The same to you, Eddie."

"Now, you can finish working on the second floor. You've probably heard a rumor that this building is going to be torn down soon. But, don't worry about your job. A new courthouse is going to be erected across the street and you'll probably just transfer over with us. For now, let's keep this old relic looking good."

"Yes, Sir. And do you think that you could possibly start me at fifteen dollars a hour now?" she pleaded. "I'm on my own."

He hesitated and thought for a few minutes. "Sure why not. It's Easter and I'm in a generous mood. I guess that I could do that. But, don't let me down."

"Thank you." She shook his hand vigorously. "Thank you."

# Chapter 3

The days and weeks flew by swiftly for Frances as she lived with Marge and Charlie and worked at the courthouse. Eddie Purdue turned out to be an extremely kind and considerate boss.

As she was promised, after three months, Frances was included on the hospitalization and dental plans with the city. Now, she could finally get her teeth cleaned and the two cavities that had long plagued her, filled.

After having saved a good amount of money, Frances decided that it was time for her to stand on her own two feet again. She found a small two bedroom apartment that she could afford that was within walking distance of the courthouse and her job.

The grubby looking and disheveled Frances that Charlie had first met, had not only changed her life, but her appearance also. A new short hairdo had replaced the long unruly locks and the strenuous maintenance work had gotten back the firm and toned body that she sported the day she had graduated from college.

A lean one-hundred and fifteen pounds now Frances was watching her weight and ate very sensibly. Even with working eight hours a days, Frances took the time to run a few miles. And with a Yankee baseball cap covering her blond hair she even competed in a couple of races in the city.

Today was to be her last regular Sunday dinner with the Marge and Charlie. While Frances was excited to be moving to her own place, the couple was sad to see her leave. She had filled a small void in their lives.

After she had lived with them for several months, Marge told

Frances about Charlie's sister. She explained that the minute Charlie had laid eyes on Frances in the courtroom, he said he could see the resemblance between her and his sister, Pauline. And he had felt Pauline was telling him to reach out and help Frances.

Marge's tone was nonchalant, but there was a sharp edge to her voice as she explained, "Pauline overdosed on sleeping pills and Charlie had a heavy heart for a long time after her death. Eventually, when we get a little older, he hopes to leave all those sad memories behind and head for Arizona. He has another sister living there and the weather will help his arthritic bones. We both love New York but the warmer climate is calling us."

After Marge related the story of Pauline, Frances felt compelled to share her personal story with Marge as they sat in the kitchen drinking a cup of coffee.

"My grandmother raised me from the time I was a baby and she was all I had. She worked hard night and day to put me through architectural school. And I never went out much or had much fun. Eventually, she passed on and I was all alone. So, the night after I graduated from architectural school, my girl friend decided to take me out to celebrate. Well, I wasn't used to drinking much and that night I got pretty drunk. We went to a club downtown, where the rock band 'Kill' was playing. I took an instant liking to the drummer in the band and the next morning I woke up to find myself in a motel room with him. Not only was I no longer a virgin; but I soon discovered I had also enjoyed sharing a lot of drugs with him. I got hooked on them and seemed to enjoy the high."

Marge's hand flew to her mouth in alarm. "Oh, my goodness," she exclaimed.

Frances squared her shoulders and continued, "Well, to make a long story short as they say, I soon found myself traveling from city to city with my drummer boyfriend and his band. I was so strung out on drugs and alcohol that I forgot all about my own career."

"How terrible." With a small and carefully placed smile curving her lips, Marge waited patiently for Frances to finish her story.

"We traveled to different clubs in many cities and were both high on drugs, music and sex. After a year with Billy, I found myself pregnant. I spent most of my pregnancy being sick in the back seat of the motor home we were traveling in." Frances realized that her voice sounded like she was on the verge of tears—which she was, but she couldn't help it.

"And the baby?" Marge asked in a whisper.

Frances managed a wan smile. "Billy knew a doctor in the town we were in when it came time for me to deliver. My baby girl was born in a small hospital in New Jersey. For the next three years, the baby and I traveled around with the band. Fortunately the drugs that I had taken while pregnant never seemed to affect the baby at all."

"That was good," Marge said, with an exaggerated sigh. "But where is your little girl now?"

"Billy and I were arrested for doing drugs in a New York City sleazy motel. The court took my baby girl away from us and placed her in foster care in the State of New York. A few days later, when we got out of jail, we jumped into the motor home and headed out with the band. About thirty miles south of New York City, the band stopped for gas. I went inside to use the rest room. When I came out, Billy, the band, and the trailer, were gone. As I stood at the curb crying, the gas station cashier walked up to me. She handed me an envelope that Billy had left for me. Inside the envelope was twenty-five dollars. All I had was the twenty-five dollars and the clothes on my back. I had no idea what to do next."

Marge could not believe the sad tale that she was hearing. She shook her head in disbelief, folded her arms across her chest and asked, "What did you do then?"

"Got a ride back to New York with a trucker. Once back in the city, I walked the streets for days looking for work. The twenty-five dollars was used for food." Frances's shoulders drooped and her whole body radiated tension. "I went cold turkey and kicked the drugs. I struggled to stay alive, working here and there and staying overnight in some creepy places. I was walking the streets, hungry and dirty and looking for work, when I was arrested and taken to Night Court, where I met Charlie."

"I'm so glad he found you and brought you to us," Marge said, taking Frances's hands in hers. She stared at Frances, her eyes pouring into her soul. She whispered softly, "And, it has been a real joy having you here."

Frances adverted her eyes. "Thanks to both of you, I think I've managed to turn my life in the right direction. My body and soul now seem to be healed. My little girl is in a home in the city and I get to visit her twice a month. Each visit, our bond is getting stronger. I've enrolled in a refresher course at architectural school and I hope one day to find a good job in that profession."

"I'm sure you will. And I know you'll get your little girl back someday," Marge added confidently.

As Frances was getting ready to leave Charlie and Marge and live on her own, she took the time to try to voice her appreciation for what they had done for her.

"I still have a long way to go. But now that my probation period is over and I have a real job, I know I'm on the way," Frances said with a quiet smile. "I'm anxious to be off on my own. You guys have been so swell and I love you both so much."

"Give us a hug," Marge ordered.

"A group hug," Charlie added.

"We have your new number and address and we'll give you a call now and then," Marge said. "We're anxious to meet your little girl. And you have to bring her around as soon as the two of you are reunited."

"Will do. I promise."

Marge gave Frances a gentle kiss on the cheek. "And who knows, maybe someday wedding bells for you." Her eyes gave away her great emotion.

Frances caught her breath and smiled gently, "Not for while. Right now, I just want to get my little girl back into my life."

"And by the way Frances, you never did tell us what your little girl's name is." Marge said.

"Leighton."

# Chapter 4

Eddie Purdue had been a true friend to Frances and helped her get adapted to her job and become part of the courthouse team. The city council had approved the money for the construction of a new up-to-date courthouse across the street from the present one. Eddie was planning to take Frances and the rest of his team to work at the new courthouse.

Frances had taken Monday morning off to move to her new apartment and to update her driver's license even though she had little use for it at the present time because she had no vehicle. Living within the city proper, she took buses and the subway every where she went.

The neighborhood around the courthouse was a residential and commercial mixture and Frances's apartment there enabled her to continue walking to work. The neighborhood was comprised of office buildings, apartments and condominiums, brownstones and small businesses like bars and restaurants. Frances was grateful that she had found a nice two bedroom, two bath apartment that was affordable to her even though it stretched her paycheck to the limits.

That afternoon, when she returned to work, Eddie told her of an opportunity to make some extra cash. Two of the offices on the upper floors of the building were looking for someone to clean their floors which he said had been sorely neglected for almost a year.

"When do they want it done?" Frances asked, her face lighting up with the thought of making extra money.

"Saturday morning," he answered.

"Say no more. I'm your gal." She smiled, her cheeks dimpling.

"I thought you would. First we have to set a time with the attorneys on the second floor. Maybe you can do the office of the architectural firm on the third floor the same day if that's agreeable with them. Follow me upstairs and I'll introduce you to the people. Maybe you'll even meet some young attorney that you could date."

Frances raised her hands as if to ward off the very thought of dating. "Not so fast, Eddie, you know my status. Money is very important to me and I'm strictly an employee here. Right now, I'm concentrating on putting my life back together and regaining custody of my daughter. So, I'm a long way from being ready to enter the dating scene. And even though you're not wearing a ring, I know you have a special someone. I saw her picture on your desk, Mr. Eddie Purdue."

"Just trying to be helpful Frances. I think you need to get out socially."

She saw what looked like genuine concern on his face. "Thanks for caring Eddie." She raised an eyebrow. She couldn't keep the determination out of her expression. "But right now, I'm concentrating on more important things. And I just finished my refresher architectural classes, so I'm focused on that too."

Entering the attorney's office on the second floor, Eddie approached the heavy set bald man, who appeared to be in his sixties, sitting at one of the desks. "Hi, Mr. Garrrison. I want you to meet Frances Taylor, one of my assistants. I told her you wanted to get your office thoroughly cleaned. She agreed to do the job on Saturday morning."

James Garrison stood up, came around his desk and walked toward Frances. "Oh yes, I've seen you working in the halls occasionally. You're the young lady who brightens up this place with her welcoming smile."

"Thank you. I try to do my best," Frances answered as she took his hand firmly in hers.

Turning to Eddie, Mr. Garrison asked, "Can you get the movers here on Saturday morning?"

"Yes. I'll arrange for them to be here about eight. They can put your desks, tables and files into the hall so Frances can do her magic and start cleaning right after the furniture is moved."

"Good. I want to get rid of the four cubicles and I need to purchase two more desks. We can use the extra space for a couple of new people I've just hired. Let's plan on doing the work Saturday morning, if that's okay with you, Frances. About seventy-five dollars for the job?"

"Sounds good to me. Thank you," Frances replied.

"You have a key to my office, Eddie, you can give her. She can start about seven in the morning," Mr. Garrison said .

"Yes, sir," Eddie replied. Turning to Frances, he asked, "This agreeable with you?"

"Perfect."

Leaving Garrison's office, Eddie turned to Frances. "Well. That seemed to go well. Let's go upstairs to the third floor. Mr. Wallace should be there now."

The Wallace Architectural Firm door was closed, so Eddie knocked briefly and entered with Frances behind him.

"Good afternoon, Mr. Wallace. This is the young lady, I told you about. Frances Taylor, please meet David Wallace."

The tall thin distinguished looking gentleman, dressed in a charcoal gray business suit with a lavender shirt and tie, stepped forward and greeted Frances warmly.

"Frances said that she would be available to do your office this Saturday," Eddie said.

Mr. Wallace was relieved to hear that. He walked around to the back of his desk and looked down at the huge calendar that almost covered the surface of the desk. "Yes. That works fine with me."

"Good. I'll call the movers and set up Saturday morning," Eddie said with satisfaction. "Now, I've got an appointment so I'll leave the two of you to work out what needs to be done in here."

After Eddie left, David motioned for Frances to sit in the chair in front of his desk. "Please have a seat, Ms. Taylor."

"Please Mr. Wallace, call me Frances."

"Thanks. I'll do that. You know, Frances, you may have a tough job cleaning this office. Four men are not very gentle on these wood floors. Sure you can handle the job?"

"Yes Sir." Frances looked down at the old dirty and scuffed floors. "It looks like you're right. But, since they're like some of the floors downstairs, I know just how to handle them."

"Great. And when you're finished, have the movers put everything back in the same place."

Frances looked around the room after he said this, thought for a few moments, then shook her head and frowned. Two large oak tables were lined up in the middle of the room and four desks and computers lined up against the walls. She looked at him pensively.

He looked at her with a perplexed expression. "Something wrong, Miss?"

She answered nervously. "It's the layout, Sir."

He frowned. "What's wrong with the layout?"

"May I have a piece of paper? I want to make a couple of suggestions for you."

Mr. Wallace handed Frances a large piece of drafting paper. "Here, use this large table to draw on." He motioned to a nearby table. "And here's a pencil."

Frances looked quickly around the room, then drew a new layout for the furniture. Mr. Wallace walked up beside her and glanced down at the drawing that she made.

"Here's my idea to make this furniture arrangement more efficient," Frances said. "First of all get rid of those large old oak tables."

"Yes. We've already purchased some new and modern drawing boards." Mr. Wallace smiled to hide his amusement at Frances' boldness.

She blushed and continued with a good deal of self assurance. "Good. I suggest they be put next to the windows where the natural light will make it easier for your staff to work. Put the desks, computers and chairs in the center of the room."

"What are these lines on your drawing?" Mr. Wallace inquired.

"Those are cubicles to separate the desks," Frances replied.

"We don't have any cubicles," Mr. Wallace said with a puzzled look.

"Please follow me downstairs to an office on the second floor. I want to show you how the lawyers have their office arranged. And, I'll bet that you can swap the four cubicles that they're planning to get rid of in return for your two desks."

Mr. Wallace followed Frances to the elevator, which they took down to the second floor.

When they arrived at the lawyer's office door, Frances knocked.

"Come in," Mr. Garrison yelled out.

"Hi Mr. Garrison. This is Mr. Wallace. He has offices upstairs and I wanted him to see the four cubicles you're going to dispose of. He might be interested in acquiring them."

"Boy. You sure work fast, young lady." Garrison's mouth twitched with a faint smile.

Mr. Wallace looked around the room at the furniture layout. "Now, I can see what you're suggesting Frances. This layout would help my staff, including my son, to concentrate more on their tasks."

"Now, Mr. Wallace, tell Mr. Garrison what you're getting rid of and could trade for the cubicle dividers."

"What do I have Frances?" he asked, somewhat bewildered.

"You have two large oak tables that you won't need any more."

"Oh, yes. The two oak tables," Mr. Wallace said, nodding his head. Turning to Mr. Garrison, he added, "I'll give you the tables in return for the four dividers, if that's agreeable with you."

Garrison grinned and thrust out his hand. "It's a deal. I was planning on moving out the cubicle dividers on Saturday morning when Frances is doing our floors. Would that work out for you?"

"Yes. That would be great. We'll have the movers make the exchange then," Wallace answered. He grinned at Frances. "Okay, young lady, let's hurry back to my office. I have a dental appointment and I want to look at your drawing more closely before I leave."

Later, as he stood staring at Frances's drawing, Wallace said, "Yes, with the tables gone, we'll have more room. Hell, we only used them to eat lunch on. I love your idea for the new and modern drafting tables. They'll fit in perfectly with the new cubicles. Much more efficient."

Frances merely smiled in return.

"Will you take charge of the re-arrangement of the furniture?" he asked.

"Of course." Frances was delighted he had so much confidence in her plan.

The door to a private adjoining office opened, and a tall, slender young man, who appeared to be in his early thirties, entered the room. His lean muscled build was clothed in an impeccably tailored suit of gray, complete with vest. Raven black hair grew thickly away from his forehead, without much thought of styling it. His eyes were the color of his hair, an intense black.

"Oh, Dad, I just wanted to tell you I'm leaving for the day. I've got a date tonight. I'm still having problems with the school layout. I left it on the table over there; but, I'll take care of it on Monday morning." His deep powerful voice sent a shiver up Frances' spine.

David Wallace looked at his son with a grimace. "Frances, this is my son, Jason. This is Frances Taylor. She's going to be cleaning our floors and re-doing our main office."

Jason glanced quickly at Frances and merely nodded his acknowledgement. "Gotta go Dad. Running late."

"Me too, Son."

As Jason started to leave the room, Frances reached out and grabbed hold of his arm. "Mr. Wallace. Jason."

"Yes?" He stopped abruptly and looked down at her.

"You said you were having trouble with your drawing of the school. Would you mind if I took a quick look at it. I've have a little architectural experience."

He grinned at her, annoyed at her suggestion. "Go for it. You can burn it for all I care. I'm starting it over on Monday."

# Chapter 5

Frances arrived at the courthouse promptly at seven on Saturday morning. After putting on her work jump suit, she grabbed her cart, cleaning equipment and some drop cloths and proceeded to the third floor. Outside of the Wallace office, she spread the drop cloths in the hallway. She strolled inside the office and opened the door to David Wallace's private office. Walking over to one of the desks, she placed a large rolled up blue print, then walked back out into the main office of the firm.

At seven-thirty, the moving men knocked at the office door. Opening it, Frances ushered the four men inside. "First of all, I need you to take the two large oak tables down to the second floor and place them in the hall outside of the Garrison law office."

One of the stout muscular men said, "Lead the way Lady. We'll follow you. You're in charge."

Lugging the oak tables one by one, the men followed Frances to the service elevator and placed the tables inside.

After taking the elevator down, Frances got off and walked down the hall to the Garrison Law office and knocked on the door. "Morning Mr. Garrison, we've brought the two oak tables. If it's okay with you, the movers will break down your cubicle dividers and remove them."

"Just have the moving men push the desks back against the far wall and put the tables in the center of the room. I'm putting a hold on having you do my floors. I think they're okay for now. Let's plan on doing them in a month or so."

"Okay with me," Frances replied. "Just let Eddie Purdue know when you want them done. He can set things up."

Frances directed the movers to take the cubicles up to the third floor and place them on the drop cloths outside the office of Wallace and Wallace Architects.

With her hands on her hips, Frances addressed the movers, "Listen fellows, help me move the rest of the furniture into the hall. Then I'd like for you to come back around noon. I should be done by then."

By eleven-thirty, Frances had the floor stripped of the old wax, cleaned and had applied a new coat of wax. Outside the office, she sat down on one of the chairs to rest. It felt good to take a break and she took several sips out of her water bottle as she reflected on the job she had just completed. She was proud of the way the old floors now gleamed with the patina of years.

Suddenly a voice called out, breaking into her thoughts. "Are you ready for us?" It was the moving men once again.

She sat up with a start and gave a self conscious laugh. "Yes. Ready to move the stuff back in."

At Frances's direction, the men moved the furniture into the office. Following her layout, she had the men set up the desks, chairs and file cabinets in the center of the work area. The drafting tables, scheduled to arrive on Monday, she planned to set up by the windows.

As she stood back and looked at the new room design with satisfaction, she felt a hand on her shoulder. She whirled around to see David Wallace standing there, looking around the room.

"My God, lady, you sure can work a miracle. The place looks better already." He sounded visibly impressed. "And I can see that each of my architects will have their own private space. We'll decide who goes where later."

"Do you like it so far?" Frances asked with an uncertain undertone in her voice.

"Like it. I love it." He laughed a great booming laugh. "With those two old tables gone, we have a lot more room already. I wish we had done this last year."

Frances sighed and released a breath of satisfaction. "Yes. And it should make the office more efficient and a nicer environment to work in."

As they were standing there admiring the new layout, Jason Wallace entered his father's private office through the hallway door. He was in the office for only a short time before he came rushing into the main drafting room.

"Hey, Dad. What's going on here?" His lips were parted in surprise. "And, look what I found on my desk. Here's a new layout for the school I was working on."

He placed it on one of the desks and rolled it open.

David Wallace studied the blue print carefully, then exclaimed, "Say, this is really good. I like it. Good work Son."

Jason smiled. "Thanks. But I didn't do it. I think that this young lady did it."

David looked puzzled. "Who did it?"

"Your cleaning lady, Ms. Taylor did it, I believe. See, it says 'F. Taylor' down here in the right hand corner of the layout."

A thrill of excitement ran along Frances' spine as the senior Wallace stared at her in astonishment.

"You did this, Frances?"he asked.

"Yes sir," she answered softly. "Your son said that it would be all right if I looked over his plans. Well, I studied them and make a few modifications."

"How did you know enough to develop this plan?"

Lifting her eyes, she replied, "You see, Mr. Wallace, I studied architecture at NYIT."

"You're an architect?" he challenged.

"Yes. And I just finished some refresher classes."

Both men stood there stunned. They could not believe this cleaning lady had actually graduated from Architectural School.

"Did you graduate and get a degree?" David asked, in disbelief.

"Yes Sir. I did."

Shaking his head, Jason turned to look at his father. "Dad, do you know what I'm thinking?"

David grinned and mischief sparkled in his eyes. "I'm way ahead of you, Son." He took a step closer to Frances. "One of our staff left this past week to move to Arizona and we were planning to look for his replacement. And I think we might have just found her."

Jason winked at Frances. "And you could work with me on the school project."

David stepped closer to Frances and took her hand in his. "Ms. Frances Taylor, how would you like to work for Wallace and Wallace Architects?"

Frances did not speak, only stared at the two as David Wallace continued, "I'll have you fill out a job application and send for a copy of your certificate. Can you start work on Monday? We'll give you a month's trial and a generous salary."

Frances made a protesting little sound in her throat. "Wait, Mr. Wallace. I work for Eddie Purdue. I can't just up and leave him."

Wallace spoke up with determination. "Don't worry, I'll take care of that. You just show up here on Monday morning at eight-thirty. Wear comfortable clothes and shoes."

Frances could not believe this turn of events. Her life was changing dramatically in just a few minutes.

David handed her a check. "Here's for your work today, Ms. Taylor. Great job getting the office cleaned up and getting everything moved back in. I can't wait to see how the new drafting tables will work out."

"We've already put the cubicles in place so they'll know how to place the tables. But, please call me Frances," she replied as she looked down at the check. "Oh, this check is too generous."

"You earned it, my Dear." David walked into his office briefly, then returned to the drafting room and handed Frances a sheet of paper. "Here's an employment application. We'll need your social security number, etc. And we can get your transcripts from NYIT. Jason will show you where you'll be working on Monday."

Jason smiled warmly. "It will be my pleasure to work side by side with you in the future, Frances. Your work looks very promising."

The next thirteen months flew by as Frances and Jason finished the school layout and the board looked for a builder.

New projects were coming into the firm all the time, and Frances was delighted to have been assigned a couple of them to work on. The reputation of Wallace and Wallace was the talk of the architectural community.

Eddie Purdue had found a new woman to take Frances's place shortly after she gave her notice. The city was still talking about tearing down the old courthouse before they replaced it with the new one. Frances had sent a letter to the city council suggesting that the city keep the old courthouse structure and suggested how the lower floors could be turned into an art museum.

Now that she was well on her way to resume her career, Frances's main concern turned to getting her little girl, Leighton, back. It had been more than four years since the state had taken her away. Frances visited her often and continued to bond with her.

Frances was now reflecting on the past few years of her life. "Well, Frances Ann Taylor, you've come a long way since graduating from college. First you wasted three years with the rock band, living on sex, booze and drugs. Then, you got dumped by Leighton's father and he just disappeared."

She told herself that it was a good thing that she met Judge Gomes in Night Court, because he had helped her get back on her feet. And someone from above had sent Charlie Strong and his wife, Marge, to assist her along the way.

The Wallace's were her guardian angels. In the past months, she had proven to them that she was a good hire. She believed her life had taken a good turn and had finally become stable.

Frances gradually became intrigued with Jason. He was obviously intelligent, well-educated and aware of what was happening in the world.

She was delighted that Jason and she had recently become very close—seeing each other daily. She loved being with him and felt that perhaps romance might now be in the air. Once a week, Jason would place a red rose on her desk.

# Chapter 6

It was now three weeks before Christmas and the streets and store windows of New York City looked like a winter wonderland. Frances had been working for months at Wallace and Wallace. She now had a full-time responsible job and a lovely apartment.

A recent article in the New York Times stated the Wallace and Wallace Architectural Firm were in contention to win the contract to design the new courthouse and that Frances Taylor and Jason Wallace were the lead architects on the project. Business was good at Wallace and Wallace. The city commission was presently waiting for the actual drawings for the anticipated court house and odds were that the bid would go to the Wallace firm.

Frances was delighted when David Wallace extended a lovely compliment to her. "You brought a new spirit to our team. And to my son also." Frances smiled, she knew that the Senior Wallace had noticed the growing affection between his son and her.

It was a cold Friday afternoon when David Wallace walked up to Frances. "It looks like the snow is going to continue all afternoon. And though it's only one o'clock, I want you to take the rest of the afternoon off. I'd like you to come in tomorrow about two in the afternoon for a special meeting. I know that it's Saturday, but something important has come up and I would like your input on it."

Frances looked up from her work, somewhat alarmed, and asked tightly, trying to sound natural, "Any problem?"

"No. And please tell Jason to see me before he leaves today."

"Sure, Mr. Wallace," she agreed, relieved. "Will do."

Before she left, she went into Jason's office to deliver the message.

"Your father is looking for you, Jason. He said that I could leave early."

As he eyed her doubtfully, she added, "As for you, my dear Jason, I'm still planning on seeing you later at my place for supper."

"Oh, I didn't forget," he assured her. "And I'm looking forward to our evening together. I'll bring some wine." He got up from his desk, walked around to the front and took both of her hands in his. "I know the office isn't a very romantic setting, but I want you to know that I've grown very fond on you." He kissed her on the cheek. "In fact, I think I've fallen in love with you."

Frances smiled and took a step closer to him, "I want you to elaborate on that statement, but not right now. Better, tell me about it later tonight when we're alone."

"Okay. You're right, dear one," Jason said, chuckling. He gave her a quick squeeze.

Before they could say any more, they saw David Wallace standing in the doorway. His voice rang out, "Jason, please step into my office. I need to talk to you at once."

"Okay, Dad." He backed away from Frances, whispering, "See you at seven. And don't worry, I won't forget the wine."

As Jason headed to his father's office, Frances grabbed her coat and galoshes and dashed out of the office, delighted to have the afternoon unexpectedly off.

She was almost floating as she descended in the elevator and left the building.

Deep in her own thoughts, she did not hear the security guard call out, "Be careful out there Miss."

After thinking briefly about how to spend her afternoon of freedom, she decided to stop by her gym for a brief work out. Might even hire a personal trainer.

"God, life is so good," she muttered to herself. Yes, she had come a long way—no more scrubbing floors—she had a real job and so many new friends. It hadn't been easy, but she had earned her new life.

When she got to the corner of West Thirty Fourth Street and

Seventh Avenue, she spotted Macy's Department Store.

"Forget the work out, girl. You need to go shopping for Christmas presents. Got to get Jason something special."

She spent over an hour in the department store, purchasing black leather gloves and expensive cologne for Jason and a muffler for his father. As she rang up Frances's purchases the clerk said, "You might want to go right home from here Miss. I heard that they're predicting four inches of snow this afternoon."

"I'll think I'll take your advice and save the rest of my shopping for another day," Frances replied. She decided she would ask Jason to go shopping with her later for gifts for his mother and her daughter, Leighton. I might even get Jason to help me put up my artificial Christmas tree tonight. Boy, that will put both of us in the spirit of the holidays, she thought.

The afternoon snow was getting more intense and the winds were swirling around the tall buildings as Frances stood at the corner, waiting for the light to change. "Time to go home girl, your holiday fun is just beginning," she whispered to herself. "And, you have to call Jason about our evening meal together. Maybe, he'll want to make it another time if the weather gets too bad. On the other hand, it probably won't stop him from coming over. At least I hope not."

Then she sighed, "I'm starting to sound like a gal who is in love. Guess, I never realized that an office romance could get so serious."

Frances noticed a man and a little girl standing in front of her at the curb. The man had his hands full of packages and was looking at the light, apparently waiting for the signal to change so they might proceed across the street. Suddenly the little girl stepped forward and started toward the other side of the street.

Out of the corner of her eye, Frances saw a taxi cab rounding the corner. It was about to hit the little girl.

Frances gasped, she paled and her eyes widened. Dropping her purse and packages, and, without a thought for her own safety, she darted toward the little girl and pushed her onto the sidewalk and out of the path of the taxi. With a screeching of brakes, the taxi came to a halt, but not before it hit Frances with its front bumper. Frances was knocked to the sidewalk and lay there stunned. Her face was ashen, contorted with pain. She had a big bump on the side of her head and a gash on her forehead that started to bleed profusely.

A crowd gathered around as she lay on the sidewalk, now unconscious. A woman ran to Frances's side, knelt and called out, "I'm a nurse. Someone call 911."

"I'm doing it now," a man's voice said. He pulled his cell phone from his pocket and dialed frantically.

The nurse whipped the scarf around her neck off and used it to firmly apply pressure to Frances's wound, trying to stop the flow of blood. Looking up at the gathering crowd, she ordered, "Get back. We need room for the paramedics."

Soon an ambulance pulled up at the curb, and the paramedics jumped out, carrying their emergency equipment. A young man rushed to Frances's side and brushed the nurse aside so that he could assess her condition.

A police car pulled up and a couple of officers jumped out and rushed over to the group that had gathered around. "Looks like this young lady took quite a hit," one of the officers said. "Who knows what happened to her?"

"She got hit by that taxi cab over there. She was trying to save that little girl." One of the bystanders pointed to the little girl standing near her father and sobbing quietly as one of the paramedics checked her over.

"What a courageous lady," one of the officers said, shaking his head. He walked over to the other paramedic and asked, "Is the little girl okay?"

"Just a cut on her knees," the paramedic responded. "Please step back."

Then the officer interviewed the father and several people in the nearby crowd as well as the taxi driver.

Shaking violently, the taxi driver said in a trembling voice, "I didn't mean to hit the lady. I didn't even see her and it happened so fast. I'm sorry."

With a compassionate look, the officer filled out his report.

After the paramedics decided she was stable, they loaded Frances into the back of the ambulance.

"Where are you going?" the nurse asked.

"We're taking her to St. Mary's Hospital. That's the closest," the paramedic responded.

Climbing into the back of the ambulance, the nurse announced, "I'm going with you."

"Wait," a young boy yelled, immerging from the crowd. "Here's the lady's purse and her packages." He handed them to the nurse as she climbed into the back of the ambulance.

The paramedics slammed the back doors shut, jumped into the front seat and with a roar, were off to St. Mary's Hospital.

Frances was rushed into the emergency room. "Hit by a taxi," one of the paramedics shouted as they wheeled her in and gently placed her on the table.

A doctor rushed over and examined Frances. "Got a pretty good gash on her head," he said as he removed the bandage the paramedics had placed on her forehead.

She started to moan and reluctantly opened her eyes. "Relax young lady," the doctor said. "Welcome back to reality. You're in good hands now."

Frances continued to moan as the doctor cut away her blouse and skirt and started to examine her body. "She has a bad bruise on her shoulder. And another one on her hip," he announced to the nurse standing nearby. "Have to put a couple of stitches in this gash."

While Frances was still only semi-conscious, the doctor numbed her wound, stitched her forehead and ordered her to be taken to the X-ray department for a complete Cat-scan.

Frances was admitted to the hospital and wheeled upstairs to a room.

Later a nurse approached her. "Well, look who finally woke up," she said, holding Frances's hand. "You've been out for quite some time."

Frances looked up at her with a puzzled expression. "Who are you? Where am I?"

"You're in St. Mary's Hospital. You got hit by a taxi and the paramedics brought you in."

"I hurt all over," she croaked, her mouth very dry.

"I'm Nurse Tillman and except for the stitches in your forehead, you appear to be okay. You also have huge bruises on your shoulder and your hip. But that's to be expected when you get hit by a taxi. Dr. Gable will be in shortly to talk to you."

Frances smiled weakly. "Thank you." Then whispered, "I have to go to the bathroom."

"Well, since you haven't got a concussion or broken bones, I can get you up," the nurse offered. "I'll grab your IV. Just hang onto me."

As Frances and the nurse returned from the visit to the bathroom, Dr. Gable walked into the room and introduced himself.

The short, pudgy man with a balding head, said with a deep voice, "Glad to see you're awake, Ms. Taylor. Fortunately, all you have are a few nasty bruises and a good gash in your forehead. I stitched it up and you shouldn't have much of a scar, if any."

"That's good. I guess that I'll live then," Frances mused.

"Yes. And hopefully, for a long time. It'll probably take several weeks for your bruises to disappear. You should come back in about ten days to get your stitches removed. You took quite a jolt to your system so I want to keep you overnight to make sure that you don't have any complications."

"Thank you, doctor." She chuckled. "It isn't often that I get hit by a taxi. But, what happened is starting to come back to me. How is the little girl that I pushed aside?"

"I've been told she is just fine. That was a very courageous thing you did. You should be fit as a fiddle in a few weeks. We can unhook your IV bag now. I'll order a light supper and a sleeping pill for you. The nurse will continue to monitor you. I expect to release you and send you home sometime tomorrow if all goes well."

# Chapter 7

Frances loved the words, "Going Home" the doctor had just said. He ordered the nurse to keep Frances comfortable and added, "I'll be seeing you again, Ms. Taylor, before you leave in the morning."

Frances smiled her gratitude as the nurse unhooked the IV bag, propped her up in the bed and left the room.

Within a few minutes, the nurse returned. "You have a couple of visitors outside, but I've instructed them to make their visits short. You need lots of rest and we don't want them to tire you out. I've ordered your evening meal for you."

"Thank you. You know, I can't remember what I had for breakfast and lunch," Frances replied brightly.

The nurse looked over her shoulder as she started to leave. "And by the way, you are the talk of the hospital for saving that little girl's life."

Feeling very humble at the praise, Frances merely smiled.

Later, Nurse Tillman opened the door to Frances's room and ushered in a tall young man, with reddish gold hair and a sprinkling of freckles covering his face and arms. The insignia on the pocket of his uniform, read "NYC Taxi Service."

He mopped his brow, his face ruddy from embarrassment. "Hi, I'm Tony McCaskill. It was my cab that hit you. I'm so sorry."

Noticing that Frances was sitting up, he added, "I'm glad to see you're looking a little bit better than I expected. I tried to stop when I saw the little girl crossing the street, I slammed on my breaks. I saw you push that little girl out of the way and then the next thing I knew you were flying through the air. I'm sorry I couldn't stop in time. I'm really a good driver, but it happened so fast." Frances could hear the anguish in his voice. He sounded as if a ton of bricks were weighing him down.

"Please Tony, I'm fine. Really. Just a little gash on my head and a couple of good bruises. No broken bones," Frances said, smiling up at him. "In fact, the doctor is going to release me from the hospital tomorrow."

Tony's anguish turned to relief. He walked over to the bed, dropped to his knees and knelt down beside Frances. He gently took her hands in his and kissed them. "I'm so glad you're not seriously hurt. My company said they'd take care of all your hospital expenses."

Frances shook her head. "That probably won't be necessary. Fortunately, I have good insurance from my job. But, thank you for offering. And don't worry, I won't hold you or your company responsible in any way. It was just an unfortunate accident and I'm thankful the little girl wasn't hurt."

Tony could hardly breathe. He gave a big sigh of gratitude, realizing that he probably wouldn't lose his job over this accident. He felt as if a heavy weight had been lifted from his shoulders. "Lady, I'm so thankful that you weren't hurt worse. You're that little girl's angel. You know miss, I haven't had an accident in over five years."

"Stop. Don't worry about anything. I'm going to be just fine. But thanks for stopping by. I really appreciate your thoughtfulness."

Tony exhaled, jumped to his feet, reached into his pocket and handed Frances a business card. "Here's my card. If you need a ride home from the hospital tomorrow or need a cab anytime in the future, please call me. No charge for you."

Frances looked briefly at the card and then placed it on the stand next to her. "Thanks. I'll remember that. And thank you again for stopping."

Shortly after Tony left her room Frances heard a brief knock on the door. "Come in," she called.

A sandy haired young man, carrying a camera, and a tall slender blonde with her makeup seemingly flawless, every strand of her perfectly coiffed bottle-blonde hair lacquered firmly in place, entered the room. In her hand she held a microphone. Behind them was a short stout elderly man, carrying a legal pad and a flash camera.

"Hi. I'm Veronica Sams and this is my camera man." Her voice was filled with self confidence. "We're from Channel Nine and would like a brief interview with you, Ms. Taylor. I realize you are probably in pain from your accident, but, I know that our viewers would like to hear from you about what happened and how you feel now. May we talk to you briefly? And this gentleman is from the local newspaper." She motioned toward the older man standing behind her.

Frances swallowed and looked startled. After thinking for a brief moment, she nodded her agreement. While Veronica asked several questions about the accident, her cameraman filmed the interview.

After they finished their interview, they thanked Frances and left the room. The newspaper man stepped forward. "I'm Bic Sloan. And, as Veronica said, I'm from The Times and I'd like a statement and some photos."

"I'm getting kind of tired. So I'd appreciate it, if you could make it fast."

"Of course," the man responded with compassion. "I can see we're tiring you."

After a short interview, Frances settled back in the bed, hoping that the newspaper man would leave.

Once again, she heard a knock on the door. She sighed, sat up and said wearily, "Come in."

A tall slender Hispanic woman with flowing black hair entered the room. Behind her were a young Hispanic man and a little girl who appeared to be about six.

"Ms. Taylor, I'm Gina Gutierrez and this is my husband, Pedro, and our daughter, Maria. God sent you to save her life. And we want to thank you because you almost lost yours in return."

Gina rushed over to Frances, leaned over and with tears in her eyes, gently kissed her on the cheek.

"Please Mrs. Gutierrez; I'm going to be all right. Don't cry."

Mr. Gutierrez stepped forward and grasped Frances' hands.

"We can't thank you enough," Mrs. Gutierrez said, as she turned to her daughter. "Maria, come over here and give your guardian angel a hug."

Maria stepped forward. Frances leaned forward to hug the little girl. "I'm so glad you're okay," Frances said, smiling at her.

Maria didn't answer. She just nodded, returned the hug and looked up at Frances with huge dark eyes.

Mrs. Gutierrez reached into her purse and pulled out a cardboard with a small pin attached to it. "We brought you an angel pin for your shoulder, so your guardian angel will watch over you all the time."

She pinned it on Frances's hospital gown.

Frances looked up at her. "Thank you. I'm sure that both your daughter's and my guardian angels were present on that corner."

Mr. Gutierrez was still somewhat shaken. Frances' statement had a ring of truth about it. He realized once again how close he had come to losing his daughter. "We don't want to tire you. So, we go. But here is a note with our address and phone number. When you get well, my wife and I would like you to come to our house for a big Mexican dinner."

"That sounds wonderful," Frances replied. She looked at Maria. "Are you sure you're okay?" she asked gently.

"My knees are scratched, but I'm okay," Maria said timidly.

Bic Sloan stepped forward. He introduced himself to Mr. and Mrs. Gutierrez and asked, "May I have a picture of your daughter and Ms. Taylor for my newspaper?"

"Just one," Mr. Gutierrez replied. "Then, we must go."

Sloan took a couple of pictures of Frances and Maria together and wrote a few notes down on his pad. The door opened and the nurse stuck her head through the doorway. "Please, everyone must leave now. Ms. Taylor needs her rest."

Within minutes, the nurse cleared the room. Looking at Frances, she said firmly, "No more visitors today. Here are your pain pills. Now, I want you to take a nice nap. I'll see you in a while."

"Thank you." Frances took her pills with a sip of water and settled back in the bed. A few minutes later, she was fast asleep.

It must have been her stomach that woke her, Frances decided a few hours later. Sitting in a chair near the window, was a woman who Frances did not recognize.

"Hi. I didn't want to wake you, so I just sat here and waited. I'm Sandy Fulton. I'm the nurse who attended to you at the accident scene and accompanied you to the hospital in the ambulance. The nurse outside told me that it was okay that I come in. She said you received several stitches to your head and that you are terribly bruised. Other than that, you're going to be fine."

Frances sat up and smiled warmly at her. "I'm so glad to meet you, Sandy. I was told you stayed with me from the time of the accident until the emergency room crew took over."

"I saw you throw yourself in front of the cab and save that little girl's life. You were extremely courageous."

Frances sent her a wry smile. "It's kind of you to say that, but I acted quickly, without thinking. Anyone would have done it."

"But you were the one who did. I brought your packages and purse along to the hospital. That's how they got all your information before they admitted you downstairs." Then she asked softly, "I guess you got your purse back?"

"Yes. Thank you. It's on the top shelf of the closet, I was told."

"Well, now that I can see for myself you are doing well, I'll run home and fix some supper for my family," Sandy said as she stood up.

"Once again, thank you for all that you did for me. I really appreciate it," Frances said, reaching out to shake Sandy's hand. "Please leave me your phone number before you leave. I'd like to take you out to lunch sometime."

Sandy pulled a card from her pocket, wrote her phone number on it and handed it to Frances. "It's a deal. Now, I've got to go."

As she left the room, Sandy whirled around. "I'm looking forward to that lunch, soon."

Curiously content, Frances settled back in the bed. Shortly after Sandy left the room, Nurse Tillman entered. She bent over and straightened Frances's bedding. "I think I can hear your stomach calling for some food. How about you hit the bathroom before I bring your supper in?"

As she helped Frances get out of bed, she could see her winch with pain. "It'll take a couple of weeks for those bruises to fade. I'll give you some more pain pills after you eat. Do you want some help in the bathroom?"

Frances was determined to be independent as quickly as possible. "No. I think that I can manage on my own."

"Well, be careful. You might still be a little weak. The night nurse will be checking on you regularly. And by the way, you had a call from someone from your office. I told them you've had enough visitors for today and need your rest. I told them to stop by in the morning."

In the bathroom, Frances stopped in front of the mirror and stared at herself. She was not a pretty sight with bandages on her forehead and the side of her face starting to turn black and blue.

"Looks like this face will take a couple of weeks to completely heal," she muttered to herself.

On the way back to bed, Frances opened the closet and reached up and got her purse. Situated in bed, she pulled out her compact and lipstick." She chuckled, "I hope my face looks better before I get any more visitors."

# Chapter 8

"Jason, how did you know I was here?" Frances exclaimed, as he entered her room early in the morning. He raced to her bedside, knelt down and threw his arms around her.

"Are you all right?" Leaning back on his heels, he asked, "How do you feel?"

Frances stiffened and laughed. "I'm feeling better this morning. Just this gash on my forehead and a few very terrific bruises. I'm on the mend now. But, how did you know I was here?"

He stood up, pulled over a chair and sat down beside her. "After you left the office, Dad and I went out together. We drove to a near-by strip mall, to look it over before we decided whether or not to purchase it. Anyway while we were there, we passed an appliance store. The television in the window had the news on. And there you were, on the evening news."

Frances interrupted with a brief laugh, "Oh, yes. Almost as soon as I got up to my room, the people from Channel Nine were here."

Jason's eyes flashed as he continued, "I went inside the store and the clerk told me what happened. You're the talk of the city and are being called a 'hero' now. So I called the hospital and got the nurses' station near your room. The nurse said you were stable and were resting. That's all she'd tell me except to say you couldn't have any more visitors last evening and I should come in this morning."

"Yes. And so you're here. Thank you for coming. Sorry I didn't call you last night and tell you what happened. I guess I just wasn't thinking too clearly."

"And you're all right? The man in the store said you saved a little girl from being killed by a taxi cab and that you got hit instead." To the casual observer, his expression would have appeared to be one of sincere concern. She was not fooled. His eyes met hers—the fear in his gaze apparent.

"Slow down, my dear. I'm doing fine. Just a small gash on my forehead and several large bruises on my shoulder and hip. I think I'm going home today. And I hope to make your Dad's meeting."

"I don't know about that. But I know I don't want to leave you ever. And, I mean never. You need me to look after you," he declared firmly.

"We'll talk about it later." She murmured, as his words resonated through her mind.  "Now, tell me why you and your father were looking at a strip mall."

"We've been looking at several properties lately. Since they're tearing down the old courthouse, eventually we'll have to find a place to move our offices. We're bidding on a building in a strip mall and we plan to be one of the tenants."

Jason leaned over, released his breath in a gusty sigh and kissed Frances. "I'm so glad I didn't lose you."

Then he looked down at her and almost started to stammer. "There's something I want to tell you. No, that's not right. There's something I want to ask you. No, that's not right. There's something I want to give you."

Jason knelt down and took Frances's left hand in his. Out of the corner of her eye, she saw him reach into the right side pocket of his jacket and pull out a small blue box.

Her mind immediately started to race in panic. "Wait a minute, Jason. Before you speak, I want you to sit on the edge of my bed. There is so much I need to tell you."

He slipped the box back into his pocket, rose up and sat down beside her. "The only thing I want to talk to you about, my dear, is our future."

Frances put two of her fingers gently across his mouth. "Please let me speak first," she commanded, as she took his hands in hers.

"Okay. Speak," he directed. "But nothing you can say will change the way I feel about you or what I'm about to ask you."

Frances shook her head. "That may not be true. You really don't know me."

A small frown touched his brow. He looked at her with concern, as her voice dropped to a whisper and she continued, "After I graduated from college, I spent a horrible three years traveling with a rock band and living with one of its members. We were into drugs and booze and that's when I had my daughter, Leighton. Her father was with the band and he and I never married. I lost custody of Leighton after he deserted me."

Jason interrupted her. "That's enough Frances. That's all in the past and all I'm interested in is our future."

"No Jason. You deserve someone better than me." Her eyes were bright with regret.

"I don't believe that for a moment," he replied indignantly. "You are one of the finest people I've ever met. And I have had problems in my past too. You see, as a child I was very spoiled. When, I grew older all I wanted to do was to party and have a good time. I barely made it through college and was lucky that I could go to work for my father. But, working with you at my side has given me a new perspective on life. Now, I know what my goal in life is and I would like to take you along. So now, my love—let me talk."

Frances sighed and sent him an affirmative smile. "Okay. If you're sure about this."

"I am," he responded, his dark eyes diamond-hard with determination. "And, well, here goes. I wish I could do this in more of a romantic setting. But, I just can't wait. When I heard you were involved in an accident, it scared the life out of me. And I prayed you'd be okay."

Frances sucked in her breath as he continued, "And it appears my prayers were answered."

Jason reached again into his side pocket and pulled out the small blue velvet box. He took Frances's right hand in his and then flipped open the lid of the box. Frances peaked inside the box and her eyes flashed as she spied a huge diamond ring.

"Frances, my love, will you marry me?"

Without any hesitation, Frances nodded her head vigorously. "Yes. Yes. But first, Dear, it goes on the left hand."

"Yes, of course," Jason grabbed her left hand and slid the ring on. He laughed. "I'm kind of new at this sort of thing."

Frances gasped and stared down at the ring. "It's perfect. The most beautiful pear shaped diamond I've ever seen."

Jason leaned forward, "Now, let's seal it with a kiss.

After a long passionate kiss, they both said, in unison, "I love you so."

"And now, I'm ready to take you home," Jason added, his voice husky with enthusiasm.

"Not just yet. The doctor said he wants to check my stitches. I should get out of here about noon."

"And how is the rest of your body?" Jason asked.

"Well, I won't show you my bruises, but I have several," Frances said, sitting up stiffly in the bed as the door opened.

They looked up and saw Jason's parents, David and Claire, enter the room. Jason jumped to his feet and rushed over to them. "She's okay. I mean Frances is okay. Just a gash in the forehead and some nasty bruises. Going home later today."

Frances greeted the Wallace's warmly as they walked over to the bed.

Jason put his arm around his mother. "Mom and Dad, I asked Frances to marry me." After a short pause, he yelled out in excitement, "And she said 'yes.' Honest she said 'yes'."

"I'm so happy for you two," Claire said, beaming at Frances. "We'll be delighted to welcome you into the family."

"Thank you." Frances breathed a sigh of relief at the woman's warmness toward her. "Would you like to see my ring," she asked, holding her hand up.

Claire took Frances's hand in hers and gazed down at the magnificent diamond.

She turned to Jason. "I always knew that you had good taste."

Her husband nodded his head. "Yes, both the ring and your

future bride are lovely."

They heard a quick knock on the door before it opened and the nurse entered. "Dr. Gable will be here soon and wants to give you a final check up. By noon, you'll be on your way."

Looking at the people standing next to the bed, she added, "I think it would be wise if you folks would give our patient the opportunity to rest for a while. She's had quite a busy morning."

The older Wallace's nodded and took a couple of steps toward the door. Jason put his arm around Frances's shoulders. "I'll be back at noon to take you home. If you feel up to it, we'll stop at the office first for a few minutes and hear about Dad's latest deal."

Frances looked over at Claire Wallace. "I have a favor to ask of you." She reached into the drawer on the stand next to her and pulled out her purse. She unzipped it and pulled out her keys. "Could you stop by my place on your way home and get some clothes to bring to me? The ones that I was wearing are all soiled and torn."

"Consider it done," Claire replied as she took the keys and put them in her pocket. Grabbing her husband by his coat sleeve, she said, "Now David, let's leave so these two can say good-bye in private. We'll be back later with your clothes, my dear."

She looked at Jason and said, "Your future bride needs her rest."

After they left, Frances stared down at the beautiful diamond on her finger trying to fully comprehend what had just happened. "I'm actually engaged to be married and to none other than my knight in shining armor," she whispered. Her mind was spinning. "Mrs. Frances Wallace—that sounds wonderful," she said aloud.

# Chapter 9

"Good morning Frances. I'm Gayle," the nurse pleasantly called out as she walked into the room. "I just came on duty."

My goodness another new face, Frances thought as she sat up. "Glad to meet you. But, I want you to tell me truthfully—how does my face look? I'll bet I really look terrible without any makeup on."

"Well, we'll take care of that before you leave. You hit the bathroom and I'll get your breakfast tray. Do you need some help?"

Frances threw back the covers and put her legs gingerly on the floor. "No. I seem to be getting stronger by the minute."

After the bathroom break, Frances decided not to return to bed. She walked over to the lounge chair in the corner of the room and sat down.

When Gayle brought the breakfast tray in, Frances gazed at it with apprehension. "Boy, I don't know if I can eat all of that. They seemed to have put a little of everything on here."

"Just eat what you can," Gayle urged. "You need your strength. I'll be back shortly."

Frances did an excellent job on cleaning up the fresh fruit, scrambled eggs and toast that was on the tray. Finally, taking a sip of coffee, she leaned back in the chair and relaxed.

Later, the door opened and Gayle entered. Looking down at the breakfast tray, she inclined her head, "Looks like you did a pretty good job on that breakfast."

"Before you leave. Let me show you my engagement ring," Frances said extending her left hand.

Gayle paused for a moment and looked down at the ring. "Gosh, that's really one magnificent diamond. It must be from that gorgeous looking man that I saw leaving earlier. What a catch!"

Frances grinned and nodded her agreement.

As she picked up the tray and turned to leave the room, Gayle added, "By the way, you have a visitor. A Mrs. Wallace. Okay if I show her in?"

"Of course." She was dismayed to learn that her future mother-in-law had been left standing in the hall.

The nurse opened the door and motioned for Claire Wallace to enter. Carrying a small suitcase, Claire looked at Frances, "I must say you're looking pretty good, considering what you've been through."

"Thank you, Mrs. Wallace," Frances conceded with a small grin.

"Please—I insist that you call me Claire. I brought you the clothes you asked for. Also, I picked up a few of your toiletries from your bathroom. What I thought you might need." She placed the suitcase on the bed. "You'll also find some clean underwear in the bottom of the suitcase." She shrugged, trying to sound casual.

Frances had a quick mental flashback. She decided she was glad she had cleaned out her closet and dresser drawers not long ago.

Claire studied her thoughtfully for a moment. "The nurse said you were going home around noon. We're planning on picking you up then. David and I will return with Jason, that is, if that's agreeable with you."

"Certainly. I'll be ready." Frances was unable to conceal her impatience. "Even though they have treated me well here, there's no place like home, as they say."

Claire took a step closer to Frances. "May I take another look at the ring Jason gave you?"

"Of course," Frances extended her left hand. After Claire looked closely, Frances drew the neck of her hospital gown aside, and added, "Oh, and I love the chain and cross that Jason gave me a couple of weeks ago."

Claire looked down at her and raised an eyebrow. "Did Jason tell you the story about the cross?"

"No. He just said that it was a family heirloom."

"Yes." Claire lifted her chin and smiled gently at her future daughter-in-law. "It was my grandmother's and she passed it down to me. In fact, my grandfather bought it for her on their honeymoon in Rome. Needless to say, it has great sentimental value to our family. When Jason told us that he was getting serious about you and was going to ask you to be his bride,  my husband suggested that I give it to Jason to pass on to you. You're going to be the next female in line for it."

"Thank you. I just love it." Frances could not believe the warmth this woman was so generously extending to her. "And, I'll plan on passing it on to my daughter."

"Yes. Jason did tell us that you had a little girl. I'm looking forward to meeting her and welcoming her into our family. Now, I've got to get going." Claire gave Frances a quick hug and turned toward the door. "Need to do a few errands. See you later."

After Claire left, Frances sat for a few moments, thinking about what had just transpired.  "Thank you God, for bringing these three precious people into my life. I'm very fortunate they are so accepting of me and my daughter."

Later, as she lay patiently in her bed, Dr. Gable entered the room. "It looks like someone is ready to go home," he said cheerfully

Frances looked up and him and smiled. "I do love the hospitality and the food here, but, I'm anxious to leave."

"First, let me check those stitches and those nasty bruises on your shoulder and thigh."

After he looked her over carefully, the doctor conceded, "Well, the bruises aren't very pretty and they'll look even worse when they turn darker in a few days. But they'll eventually fade away. In the meantime, you have to keep the stitches dry. I would suggest taking a bath or pulling a shower cap, down over your forehead if you shower."

"I'll be sure to do that," Frances promised.

"Good, I'll sign your release papers on my way out and the nurse will be in with a list of follow up instructions. I'll see you in about ten days." Dr. Gable stood up and headed for the door.

A short time after the doctor left, Nurse Gayle returned. "Okay, now it's magic time. I'll take you down to the shower room and get you cleaned up before you leave."

"Dr. Gable said to be sure to keep my stitches dry," Frances said.

"That's why we keep a good supply of shower caps on hand. After the shower, I'll help you get dressed, so that your Prince Charming can whisk you away."

"Thank you. I expect my fiancé, Jason, and his parents around noon. And he really is my Prince Charming. I can't imagine marrying a more thoughtful and caring man."

Gayle laughed. "I got pretty lucky myself. My husband, Joe, and I will be married  twenty-five years this month. Not too many couples even bother to get married these days."

After placing Frances in a wheelchair, Gayle took her down the hall to the shower room and helped her bathe and carefully washed her hair.

I never knew that a shower could feel so good, Frances thought on the way back to her room. Except for the cut on the head and a few bruises, I feel like a million bucks now.

Back in the room, Gayle put Frances's suitcase on the top of a nearby chair and opened it. She removed the clean undergarments and helped Frances put them on. Then, she pulled out a black business suit, a white lacy blouse and some low heeled black pumps. "What no jeans and T shirt?" Gayle asked.

Frances frowned. "You're right. Where did Mrs. Wallace think I was going?"

After getting dressed, Frances sat down on the edge of the bed and said to Gayle, "Now for my face.  I'm glad Mrs. Wallace remembered to bring my make-up case. I want to look extra pretty when my fiancé arrives. And I'm thankful that I took a class at Macy's on how to apply my make up properly. The class was free, but I spent a bundle on the cosmetics—eyebrow pencils, brushes and the makeup itself."

After she finished putting on her makeup, Frances leaned back and looked at herself carefully in the mirror. "Considering what I've been through, I guess I don't look too bad."

"Personally, I think you look marvelous," Gayle bubbled with enthusiasm. "You just need to slip on your shoes and you'll be ready to go."

They heard a couple of quick taps on the door and Gayle stepped forward and opened it. Standing in the doorway were Mr. and Mrs. Wallace. Behind them, with a big bouquet of pink roses in his hands, was Jason.

Jason scurried across the room, leaned over, kissed Frances and handed her the bouquet. Looking over his shoulder, he said, "You see Mom and Dad, I did pick out the most beautiful girl in the world."

David Wallace chuckled, "Next to your Mom, she comes in a close second."

Jason glared at his father. "I think you've become prejudice over the years."

His mother's lips twitched with the need to laugh. "No, Jason. He's just been trained to say the right thing when I'm around." She put her arm around her husband's waist.

He leaned over. "Now quit your fussing my dear and give me a hug."

She smiled good-naturally and did as she was instructed. "Now, gentlemen, let's take this lovely young lady out for her big surprise."

Frances's head went up at that comment. "Surprise? What, where, and when?"

"You'll see the what and when soon. The where is at the office," Jason replied.

"Maybe this is why your mother brought me this business suit just to wear to the office?"

"Yes, Frances," Claire said, smiling. "My husband has some big news for you."

"What is it?" Frances asked with anticipation.

"You'll see soon enough," a grinning David Wallace answered.

A short while later, Gayle brought in the discharge papers and the list of instructions for Frances's follow-up care. After signing them, Frances was placed in a wheelchair and Gayle, with Jason and his parents following behind, wheeled her down the hall toward the elevator.

As she passed them, Frances bid the staff good-bye, thanked them for excellent care and gave them a final salute.

On the way down in the elevator, Claire reached into her pocket and pulled out a black beret. "I saw this in the store after I left you earlier. And it seemed to call out to me. I thought you might like this to cover your stitches."

She put it on Frances, pulling it down just far enough to conceal the stitches. Looking down at Frances, she added huskily, "Very chic. With your black suit and pumps, you look like you just stepped out of a shop in Paris."

Frances was very touched. "Thank you Claire, for your thoughtfulness. I really appreciate it."

When they got downstairs, Jason brought the car up to the door of the building. His parents got in the back of the car, while he helped Frances into the front passenger seat. "Now, on to our next destination."

# Chapter 10

"Let's get going Jason," David Wallace said as he sat down in the back seat of the car next to his wife. He tapped Frances on the shoulder. "You sure do look stylish in that beret. You look like you're ready to head for Europe on your honeymoon."

Frances turned her head, looked over at Jason and grinned at him as he drove out of the hospital parking lot. "First, maybe we should get married, then the honeymoon." Then drawing in a deep breath, she added, "The fresh air does smell so good. I wouldn't want to stay in that hospital for a long period of time."

As Jason pulled into the parking garage of the courthouse, his father leaned forward in his seat and asked, "I hope that the two of you haven't forgotten our meeting today?"

"No we haven't forgotten," Jason replied. Then glancing over at Frances, he asked, "I hope you're up to it, Dear."

"I'm feeling fine." Looking over her shoulder at the senior Wallace, she questioned, "Why all the secrecy? You aren't planning on laying me off are you?"

David Wallace smiled and didn't answer. Frances's curiosity ratcheted even higher.

Jason parked the car and they exited and walked to the door leading to the inside of the courthouse. After Jason rang the bell several times, the security guard opened the door. "Afternoon, folks. Oh, Mr. Wallace, the location of your meeting has been changed. Everyone is waiting for you in room, one-ten."

Then looking at Frances, he added, "I saw you on television, Miss. I must say you look pretty good considering what you went through.

It's amazing to believe you risked your life for that little girl. You are one courageous lady."

"Thank you," Frances replied, accepting the praise with reluctance. Looking at David Wallace, she asked, "I thought we were going to the office, Mr. Wallace"

"Just follow me, my dear. Just follow me," he responded.

Jason took Frances by the hand. "Boy are you in for a surprise."

As they entered room one-ten, Frances saw several people seated around a long table. Judge Harold Gomes was sitting at one end and standing behind him was Charlie Strong.

When the judge saw them enter, he pointed to chairs in front of the table. "Please folks, take a seat," he instructed.

Seated on the other side of the table were two women and a man. On their right, was a large red-faced man with sparse gray hair and a bushy mustache. Spread out on the table in front of him was a large stack of papers.

Frances was very hesitant as she gingerly sat down. Jason and his parents took the seats next to her.

The judge leaned over the table and smiled at Frances. "Don't worry, Ms. Taylor, all is good. You have been brought here at the request of your employer, David Wallace. Mr. Wallace has had Attorney Cunningham file papers on your behalf to regain custody of your little girl." His words carried a very serious tone as he gestured toward the red-faced man.

Frances stared at the Wallaces in amazement. "Is that true, Jason?"

"Yes. Its Dad's surprise," he replied, taking her hand in his.

The judge looked over at Frances. "Of course, you remember Charlie Strong."

Frances waved her hand at Charlie. "Good to see you again, Charlie."

"Same here. It's your big day," Charlie replied.

The judge added, "And seated across from you are the representatives from the child welfare board. They're here to ask you a couple of questions and to help me to decide on your application for permanent custody of your daughter."

"Yes, Sir. I mean yes, your Honor," Frances responded softly.

"And you probably know the board members?" the judge asked. He nodded toward the three.

"Yes. I talked with them a couple of times when I visited my daughter."

The Judge gazed at the board members. "Mrs. Gardner, do you have any questions to ask Ms. Taylor at this time?"

A middle aged lady with horn rimmed glasses looked up from her papers. "Just one question. It says here you and the child's father were never married." She lifted her brows in distain. "Do you know where he is at this time?"

Frances cleared her throat. "Billy Knight is her father. After he moved to California, he was arrested with his friends for a store robbery. He was sentenced to twenty-five years in prison and is still there. I talked with the warden at the prison not long ago and he said that Billy recently lost his appeal for early release."

Attorney Cunningham looked up. "Your honor, at the request of the Wallaces, I have contacted Mr. Knight and he has agreed to give up all parental rights to the child." He reached into the pile of papers in front of him. "Here is the agreement that he signed and returned to me."

"Charlie, please bring the paper to me," the judge instructed. Looking at the other two board members, he asked, "Mrs. Wagner and Mr. Kline, do you have any questions or comments for Ms. Taylor at this time?"

Mr. Kline, a man with gray hair and penetrating charcoal eyes, nodded. "Ms. Taylor, I saw on television where you saved a little girl from almost certain death, by throwing yourself in front of a taxi. I just wanted to commend you on your courageous act of heroism. How are you doing?"

Frances took off her beret and pushed her hair to the side. "Just a few stitches here in my forehead, but the doctor said it wouldn't leave a scar. Also some bruises on my arm and hip. I expect to return to work next week."

"Well, Ms. Taylor that is good news. I just have a couple of more questions for you. How do you plan to support the child and where do you plan to rear her?"

Frances stood up. "First of all, Sir, I've been employed at Wallace and Wallace Architectural Firm for almost a year. Presently I reside in a nice two bedroom apartment about a block from a private school where I can enroll Leighton. And Jason Wallace just asked me to marry him. We plan to marry soon and Leighton will have a true father." She lifted her head high. "So you see, the future looks very bright for us."

She smiled at Jason, who quickly jumped to his feet and took France's hands in his. "And right after the wedding I plan to adopt Leighton."

Her eyes filling with tears, Frances put her head on his shoulder. "Thank you. I love you."

As they sat back down, Frances looked over at Claire and whispered, "Now, I realize why you brought me a nice business suit to wear today, instead of jeans and a shirt."

Judge Gomes smiled and said, "Let's return to the business of the day. Unless the board has any more questions or objections, I am prepared to make a decision on the motion before me."

He peered over at the board members, who shook their heads.

Looking down at Frances with a thoughtful smile, he said, "I decree that Leighton Ann Taylor be restored to the custody of her natural mother. The father has given up his parental rights and will no longer have a say in the raising of the young lady. This will also relieve him of paying any future child support."

Frances jumped to her feet and started to cry with joy. She turned to Jason and hugged him excitedly as the rest of the people in the room applauded.

"Bailiff, please bring Leighton Ann Taylor into the courtroom," the judge ordered.

Grinning from ear to ear, Charlie, said loudly, "My pleasure, Judge."

Charlie stepped out of the courtroom and returned seconds later with Leighton, a delicate blonde haired five-year-old child. When she saw her mother standing by the table, Leighton ran to her and threw her arms around her waist and hugged her tightly. Both of them sobbed quietly, tears running down their cheeks.

As she sat down and pulled Leighton onto her lap, Frances looked at Jason. "Thank you. I've waited so long for this moment."

Leighton leaned closer to her mother and asked, her eyes huge, "Mommy, can I go home with you now?"

"Yes, yes." Frances whispered. "And I'll never let you go again."

The judge looked over at them and smiled broadly. "This meeting is now over. Ms. Taylor, please sign the papers the court has prepared for you before you leave."

Everyone jumped to their feet and gathered around Frances and Leighton, exclaiming their elation over the judge's decision.

Leighton put her arms around Frances's waist and leaned her head against her. "Mommy, you look so beautiful."

"It's you that brings the glow to my face." Frances turned Leighton towards Jason. "Honey, this is my very special friend, Jason. He and I are going to be married soon and he will be your daddy."

Jason shook Leighton's hand. "Very glad to meet you, Leighton. And after your mommy and I get married, I hope that you will be happy in your new home with us."

"Will I have my own room?" Leighton asked excitedly.

"Yes. And you can decorate it any way you wish."

"Oh, that would be wonderful," Leighton responded.

Frances drew Leighton toward David and Claire Wallace. "This is Jason's parents, Mr. and Mrs. Wallace. Mr. Wallace is the man that mommy works for."

Turning to look at the judge who had just walked up to her, Frances said, "Thank you, so much Judge Gomes for all you have done for me."

"Hey, you proved to everyone that you deserve to have your daughter back in your life. And you have shown me a second chance can really work out for some people."

Charlie walked up and threw his arms around Frances and

congratulated her. Then, looking down at Leighton, he added, "Don't you let your mother forget to bring you to visit me and my wife."

After signing the legal papers giving her permanent custody of her daughter, Frances linked arms with Jason and Leighton. Looking at Jason's parents, Frances exclaimed, "Mr. and Mrs. Wallace, I will be eternally grateful to you for all you have done for Leighton and me."

"Believe me, you deserve it," David Wallace replied earnestly.

Leighton tugged at Frances's coat. "Now, can we leave? I want to see my new bedroom."

Jason looked at Leighton and grinned. "Good idea. But, I would like to make a quick stop before I take you and mommy home. Is that okay?"

"Is it a surprise?" Leighton asked excitedly.

"Kind of. How about I take you and your mother out for an ice cream sundae or maybe even a banana split?"

Leighton jumped up and down with excitement. "Can we? Can we please, Mommy?"

Frances sighed and looked down at her daughter in contentment. "Of course, my sweet little girl."

Jason and Frances each took Leighton by a hand. With Leighton walking in the middle, they exited the building. Leighton looked up at Frances and asked, "Now, we're a real family. Right Mommy?"

Frances's face broke into a big smile. "Yes, we're a real family."

# Make Me Beautiful

## Chapter 1

"Nurse. Nurse. Doctor. Doctor! Where the Hell is everyone?" Harriett Kincaid called out as she laid in the hospital recovery room. "I want to see my baby. Damnit! Someone help me!"

"Please Ms. Kincaid. I'll be with you in a moment," the nurse called from across the room. "Right now, we're attending to your baby."

"Why won't someone bring me my baby?" Harriett demanded.

Harriett was tall and thin and in her late thirties. Her face was lined with wrinkles—perhaps from the hard life she had experienced. Finding herself unexpectedly pregnant at this age, she felt she was too old to be changing diapers. She had thought momentarily about having an abortion before she discovered it was too late. She had to accept the fact she was going to be a mother for the first time. She wasn't at peace with the thought, neither was she at war with herself over the idea. She was simply resigned to the fact.

"Patience Dear," the nurse responded.

A doctor, still clad in his delivery room scrubs, appeared at Harriett's side. "Good morning, Ms. Kincaid. I'm Doctor Lassiter." At fifty-nine, Lassiter looked much younger with just a tiny bit of gray around the temples showing from underneath his surgery room cap. "Your regular doctor is out of town and they called me in to help with the delivery."

"Where's my kid?" Harriett asked sharply.

"The nurse will bring you your baby in just a few minutes. As you probably recall, you were having a tough time delivering naturally. So we had to put you under and take the baby caesarean. I'm happy to say you have a healthy seven pound baby girl. But, let me explain something before you see your baby."

"Give me my kid. Let me hold her," Harriett demanded.

The nurse brought the little baby, wrapped in a receiving blanket, over and laid her on Harriett's chest. Harriett looked down and noticing a large purple mark down the right side of her face, she screamed out, "Her face! Her face! What's that on her face?"

"It's just a small birthmark," the doctor answered.

"Small!" Harriett exclaimed. Anger and frustration balled in her chest until she thought she might explode with it. "It covers almost the whole side of her face—from her eye down to her mouth! She's hideous! She's not my child. You did this with the C-section. I'm going to sue this hospital. Take this ugly thing away."

For a moment the doctor said nothing, and then let out a frustrated breath. "Calm down, Ms. Kincaid. This is something that just happens occasionally in nature. This had nothing to do with the delivery," the doctor stated firmly. "Perhaps, as she gets older, something can be done to partially remove her birth mark."

"Well, damnit it. Take the baby away." Harriet lifted her chin arrogantly. "She's ugly. I can't let anyone see her."

After she came out of the recovery room, Harriett was wheeled to a regular room, where the nurse assigned to her introduced herself. "Good afternoon, I'm Nurse Sara Atkins and I'll be caring for you."

Sara was a beautiful young woman. She appeared to be half American Indian and half Mexican. She had dark hair and eyes and an exotic high-cheek-boned face. Having heard that Harriett's baby was disfigured, Sara's voice was full of compassion as she asked, "Would you like to try to nurse the baby now, Ms. Kincaid?"

"No. No. I can't stand to see that repulsive thing now. Much less try to feed her."

Sara arched her eye brows, shocked. Then her voice assumed a harsher tone, "Sooner or later, Ms. Kincaid, you're going to have to deal with this issue. The baby is yours and she is your responsibility."

Harriett swore, frustrated by the circumstances, by the responsibility that had been forced upon her. "I need to get my strength back before I can decide what to do with her. Right now, please leave me alone." Anger at her situation surged through Harriett—an almost irrational anger.

Sara shrugged her shoulders in dismay as she pulled a tall writing table closer to the bed. "Before I can give you something to calm you down and let you go to sleep, we need to fill out some paperwork."

Harriett glared at her, irritation naked in her eyes. "Let's get it over with, so I can rest."

"First. The birth certificate. Who shall we list as the baby's father?"

"Don't know and don't care," Harriett replied. "Could be any one of several bastards who knocked me up."

Sara cringed and continued. "Let's see what the delivery room put down on the chart. Weight; seven pounds. Height; twenty-one inches." Then with a question in her voice, she asked, "Race?"

"White, of course," Harriett responded. In a very sarcastic voice, she added, "You don't think I would sleep with any blacks or Mexicans do you?"

Sara took an involuntary step back at this remark, as if Harriett had slapped her, her face going white. Personally insulted and hurt to the core, Sara caught her breath. "Please Ms. Kincaid, let's try to finish this so you can rest. How about a name for your beautiful little girl?"

Harriett laughed cynically. "She's certainly not beautiful to me."

"You have to name her," Sara responded firmly.

Harriett shrugged her shoulders. "Okay, let's call her Katherine Ann—that was my mother's name." Then she added, bitterly, "Not that she was much of a mother."

"Well, hopefully, you can be a better mother to your daughter than yours was to you."

"Maybe. Are we done now?"

Unable to deal with Harriett's anger any further, Sara stared at her feet, then nodded and walked over to the IV that had been inserted in Harriett's arm in the delivery room. "I'm adding a nice sedative to your IV now. You should be able to sleep now."

Three hours later, Nurse Sara tapped Harriett gently on the shoulder. "Wake up, Ms. Kincaid. Your supper is here. I've got some soup and a chicken pot pie for you. That should be gentle on the stomach after your surgery."

"First, I have to go to the bathroom," Harriett responded grumpily.

With the IV still in Harriett's arm, Sara helped her out of bed and to the bathroom. "By the way, did you change your mind about nursing the baby? It would be easier for you and healthier for her."

"No. I still don't want to nurse her." Harriett clenched her fingers into fists.

"Do you wish to at least see her now?"

At this question, Harriett flushed, obviously angry. "Later. Right now I'm hungry."

As she was finishing her supper, Harriett heard a brief knock on the hospital room door. The door opened and a lady stuck her head inside. "Hi, Harriett, it's your favorite neighbor, Phyllis Green."

Harriett looked up. "Nice of you to come, Phyllis. But not necessary."

Phyllis was a stout, older woman with gray hair, cut in a short bob. She wore glasses with half lenses, over which she peered. She managed to give an impression of polite deference. Phyllis walked over to the bed and gave Harriett a hug.

Phyllis sensed in Harriett a deep need for love and companionship, loneliness so sharp that she could almost feel it. "Of course it's necessary. What kind of a friend would I be if I didn't rush over to see you and the new baby?"

Harriett looked dejected. "I don't wish to talk about the baby." She made a sound of frustration and anger and dragged a hand through her hair. "It's a girl, by the way and she is horribly deformed. I'm planning to put her up for adoption."

"What do you mean deformed?" Phyllis asked, her voice filled with compassion.

"She has an ugly birthmark running down the whole side of her face."

Phyllis glared at Harriett with an indignant look. "Harriett, lots of babies are born with birthmarks. As she gets older, I'm certain the doctors can do something to remove it, or make it less visible."

Harriett stared at her with doubt. "Do you really think so?"

"Of course. And as your neighbor and best friend, I want the two of you to move in with me. I have an extra room and I would love the company. That way we can take care of your baby together. Anyway, now that I'm retired I need something to do. Everything will be fine, I promise you. I remember when I was sick, you were there for me. And who says that two ladies can't take care of a child? We can certainly give her lots of love."

Harriett contemplated that thought for a long time, then sighed and said, "That's very kind of you. And, if you think we can do this together, I'll give it a try."

"I'm certain we can. Have you named her yet?"

"Yes. Katherine Ann."

"That's a lovely name. I'll have to leave now. My niece has a lot of baby furniture we can borrow. I'll turn the back bedroom into a nursery for the baby. And I'll purchase some baby bottles, formula and a few other things. Call me when you're ready to come home."

# Chapter 2

Thanks to Phyllis, who promised to help raise the baby, it was not quite so difficult for Harriett to accept Katherine. It did not take Harriett long to move her belongings to Phyllis's apartment where she and baby Katherine would share the second bedroom.

It took Harriett several weeks to recover from the caesarean, because the doctors discovered she had fibroid tumors in her uterus. Ultimately, the doctors decided to do a complete hysterectomy. This did not upset Harriett because she realized she would not have to worry about getting pregnant again and could resume her old carefree lifestyle. Eventually Harriett sold her house and used most of the money to pay off her hospital and doctor bills.

To Phyllis's dismay, Harriett spent little time with the care of young Katherine. Harriett applied for and got a job working from eleven until seven a.m. in the basement laundry room of St. Regis Hospital.

Her days would be spent sleeping. Before she would start her work shift, Harriett would hang out at "Charlie's Bar," drinking, partying and meeting all kinds of unsavory men. All this time, Phyllis lovingly took over the duties of caring for the baby.

It would be Phyllis Green who would take Katherine to the doctors and dentists over the years. Harriett was grateful to be working the night shift full time where she received benefits.

As Katherine started to get older, Phyllis realized the child's education was important and that once she was grown, she would have to adapt to the everyday world.

"How are we going to educate our little girl?" she asked Harriett.

"Well, you graduated from college. Maybe you can home school her. I just can't stand the thought of people staring at her. Other children would make fun of her. Maybe you could just home school her until we can see about getting her birthmark removed."

Phyllis's eyes narrowed. Her voice was sharp and cross as she snapped, "That takes a lot of money, Harriett. Something we haven't got right now." Her outburst had relieved some of the repressed resentment which had roiled inside her over Harriet's indifference to the child's suppressed lifestyle.

Harriett retorted, sounding irritated. "I know. Right now, I need to buy new winter coats for both Katherine and myself. The weatherman said Philadelphia is going to have a brutal winter."

Then she mused out loud, "Maybe I should buy a damn lotto ticket. That way all our money worries would be over."

Phyllis glared at her—resentment flickered in her eyes. "No. You would just be wasting your money. Money we need to live on. Right now we're living comfortably on what we have but you need to stop wasting money on the bar scene and spend more time with your child."

"Okay, I promise," Harriet replied, snubbing out her cigarette. "But for now, please no lectures, just do me a favor and plan on home schooling her."

"I love that little girl so much, there's nothing I wouldn't do for her." Phyllis narrowed her gaze at Harriett contemptuously. "We should just be grateful she's so bright and healthy. I'll stop by one of the near-by schools and see if I can get information on home schooling."

"Thank you, "Harriett replied as she gave Phyllis a hug. "Someday I'll show you my gratitude for all you're doing for us."

At Harriett's orders, little Katherine spent almost all of her time inside of Phyllis's apartment as Harriett did not want anyone outside to see her deformed child. Late night grocery shopping and going to the six a.m. mass on Sundays with Phyllis was Katherine's only time out of the house. In church, they sat in the last pew, so as not to be noticed.

While Katherine seemed unaware of her isolation, on many occasions, Phyllis said to Harriett, "You know my friend, you can't keep Katherine isolated forever. Right now, she seems content spending her time watching television and reading her books, but she does need the companionship of other children, in order to learn to socialize with her peers."

Harriett responded indignantly, "Please Phyllis, right now, let's keep the arrangement we have. Let's wait until Katherine is in her teens to have her associate with others her age."

Phyllis sighed, her gaze remained disapproving. "Well, okay for now. But you can't keep her locked up forever."

When Katherine turned six, the birth mark still covered the right side of her face and was too big to cover up adequately with her hair. Since having been told when the little girl was very young that the treatment for the birthmark would be very expensive, Harriett had ignored Katherine's situation. She knew she simply did not have the money.

Somehow, Katherine never questioned her deformity, but rather managed to keep her spirits high and positive. "You know Momma, someday, I'm going to be a nurse and work at the hospital where you work."

"Yes Dear. Someday," Harriett answered. When Katherine reached the age that most children started to attend kindergarten, Harriett refused to send her to school. Instead, Phyllis got all the materials needed to home school the young girl for the next eight years.

"I'll do the best I can to see she's well educated," Phyllis said determinedly. "She'll be one of the smartest kids around, if I have anything to do about it."

And from that time on, Phyllis worked with Katherine daily, devoting herself to giving Katherine the best education she could.

When she got older, Katherine spent many of her evenings at the local library, reading various books she was drawn to with fascination. Librarian Judy Hunter taught Katherine all the aspects of obtaining information from the library and Katherine soaked up knowledge like a sponge.

When Katherine was ready to start high school, Phyllis refused to home school her any further. She told Harriett that Katherine had already progressed past the stage where she could provide her with an adequate education and she insisted that Harriett send Katherine to a regular school.

Harriett finally agreed to enroll Katherine in a small high school where a lot of the teachers volunteered extra time to the students. Once she started school, Katherine soon discovered Phyllis's home schooling had provided her with knowledge far above most of her fellow students.

None of her class mates seemed to care about Katherine's birth mark. Most of them had their own problems to deal with. Katherine discovered going to public school offered her social challenges with her peers she was not accustomed to. She thrived and became an excellent student. Eventually, some of the other students wanted to be her friend so she could assist them with their studies.

When Katherine got old enough to get a part-time job, Judy helped her obtain a position cleaning the library at night. Katherine would save every cent she earned in hopes of one day getting her birthmark removed.

While Katherine was in high school, Harriett continued to work nights in the hospital laundry because it provided higher wages than the day shift. Now that she was quite a bit older, Harriett was not so keen on seeking the wilder side of life and gradually grew closer to her daughter.

Even though she had good health insurance from the hospital, Harriett learned it would not cover the entire cost of the numerous laser treatments that would be required to correct Katherine's birthmark. Dealing with everyday expenses, her wages were not enough to cover the cost of the insurance co-pays. So once again, there was no thought of trying to get Katherine's condition corrected.

Both Phyllis and Harriett were delighted when Katherine graduated as valedictorian of her high school class. Katherine told everyone her objective for the future was to get a degree in nursing.

However, at the present time their economic condition prevented her from enrolling in college full time.

Instead, Katherine was content with accepting a night time job working with her mother in the hospital's laundry and taking classes during the day at the local college.

She was so determined to get ahead that she would not allow anything to dampen her spirits.

She was disappointed to learn her mother was once again drinking. Occasionally, Harriett had to just sit and rest while at work, and without hesitation, Katherine would say, "If you don't feel good, Momma, I can finish for you this evening."

Harriett's voice was thick with guilt. "You are such a good girl. And someday, we'll get that birthmark removed and you can take your rightful place in the world and show everyone what a wonderful person you are."

Katherine would merely nod her head sadly in acceptance of her circumstances. She had no illusions of getting her birthmark removed any time soon. She realized she had to just concentrate on helping her mother and Phyllis with the everyday expenses. Any treatment would have to be considered in the far future.

"Can you finish up by yourself tonight, "Harriett asked one evening. "I'm a little tired."

Katherine could see once again her mother had too much to drink before they started their shift. She quietly answered, "Sure, you go home. I'll manage."

It was close to one in the morning, when the phone in the laundry room rang incessantly.

"Laundry department. Katherine Kincaid speaking. Who's calling?"

"This is the head nurse in surgery. We have a problem."

# Chapter 3

"What's that?" Katherine asked with a sense of trepidation.

"One of our surgeons lost his wallet. We looked all over for it up here. We thought it might have dropped into one of the laundry carts with some of the soiled towels."

"I was just about to call upstairs," Katherine replied with some satisfaction. "When I started to put a load into one of the washers a billfold did drop out. It belongs to a Dr. Freeland."

"My goodness, are you sure?"

"Yes," Katherine answered. "I looked through it and found a driver's license. It says Dr. Jonathan Freeland."

There was a pause on the other end of the line and Katherine could hear the nurse say a few words to someone. Then, she spoke again, "Hold on please. Dr. Freeland is right here."

"Miss. The nurse says you found my wallet in the dirty towels. Can you hold onto it for a few minutes? I'll be right down to get it. How do I find the laundry room? I've never been there." Katherine could hear the relief in his voice.

"Where are you now, doctor?" Katherine asked.

"I'm still in the operating center."

"Just go to the end of the hall and take the service elevator down to the basement. Once you get downstairs, take the hall to the left. The laundry room is at the end of that hall."

"Don't move lady," Dr. Freeland ordered. "I'm on my way."

A short time later, he opened the double doors leading into the laundry room and stepped inside.

Hearing his footsteps, Katherine called out, "Over here, Doctor."

She was standing in the shadows next to the row of dryers that lined the back wall.

As he approached her, all Dr. Freeland could see was her silhouette in the dark shadows. A little annoyed, he asked sharply, "Why is it so dark in here?"

"Light problem. Maintenance is supposed to come and replace a couple of fluorescent tubes, but I don't think anyone's working tonight," Katherine replied. She was used to everyday inconveniences.

"Now, Katherine, how did you find my billfold? Your name is Katherine, I believe," he asked as he edged nearer to her.

Jonathan Freeland was six feet two, strong and athletic looking with dark hair, intense blue eyes and a slight stubble on his jaw line. He took Katherine's breath away with his brooding dark looks and there was something magnetic about him, something incredibly masculine.

When he got closer to her, Dr. Freeland could not believe how stunning this young woman was. Of slightly more than medium height, she had long red hair, styled in a sophisticated chignon. Her face was a classic cameo-like oval, with dark brown eyes, a dainty nose and a sweet rosebud of a mouth.

Suddenly, she turned the right side of her face toward him. He saw that her perfect beauty was marred by a horrible deep red birthmark which covered the right side of her face from the corner of her eye down to her chin.

"Yes. I'm Katherine Kincaid. My mother is the laundry department supervisor. And I usually work nights. Your billfold fell out of one of the bundles of dirty towels send down from surgery. I'm sorry I had to look inside your billfold, but I wanted to find out who it belonged to." Katherine reached into her pocket and handed it to the doctor.

Dr. Freeland took the billfold and looked through it briefly.

Katherine took a sharp step back. Her mouth thinned. "Oh, I didn't take anything out of it. Honest!"

"I didn't think you did. You're a life saver." He smiled reassuringly at her. "I would hate to have to call my credit card companies. That's a real pain in the you-know-what. I'm headed to California in a few days and I'll need my driver's license to get on the plane. So thank you, so much."

He reached into the billfold and pulled out a couple of bills. "I want to give you a reward for finding my wallet."

Katherine took a step closer to him—almost insulted that he had offered her money. She shook her head. Her voice was almost shrill. "Please Doctor, I was just doing my job. I'm glad you and your wallet are back together."

Dr. Freeland was taken aback. He realized he had almost insulted this proud young woman. He was extremely curious to learn more about her and decided to quickly change the subject. "Do you plan to do this laundry job as a career?"

"No, this is just temporary. I plan to attend school when I have enough money saved. I hope one day to become a nurse."

She stepped closer to the folding table in the center of the room. "Gotta get back to work, so you'll have to excuse me. I'm all alone tonight since my mother went home sick. You can head back down the hall to the service elevator and take that upstairs."

Now that Katherine was standing under the overhead light that shone down on the folding table, the doctor got a good look at her face and the hideous birthmark. He stepped closer to her. Cautiously, he asked, "You were born with that birthmark. Right?"

Katherine's back stiffened. "Yes. I hope one day to be able to afford treatment to get it removed." Her voice was not filled with remorse. She was too proud for that.

Dr. Freeland pulled a small camera out of his pocket. "If you don't mind, I'd like to take a photo of that birthmark. I might know of someone who could help you."

Katherine looked at him doubtfully and nodded her consent.

After taking the photo, the doctor turned and left the room. When he was gone, Katherine glanced at the old clock on the wall. "Looks like I'm going to be here late tonight."

Upstairs, outside of the surgery center, Dr. Freeland found his operating partner, Dr. Timothy Simms, cleaning up after an operation.

Dr. Simms was considerably shorter than Jonathan Freeland; but, he had a stocky athletic body and a slightly toothy grin—and an amazing mane of sandy-colored hair.

"Go out with me Simms, I need a drink," Dr. Freeland said.

"My God, man, it's one in the morning," Dr. Simms said. "But, Hell, I may need two drinks It's been a long day."

"You got that right. I must tell you about my lost wallet and the young lady who found it."

"When we get to the bar, you can tell me about her. But first, I'd like to go over our plans for California." Dr. Simms took Dr. Freeland's arm and headed out the door to Maisie's Tavern.

# Chapter 4

"Maisie, I need two bourbon and waters, at once," Dr. Simms said to the bartender as they took their seats at the bar. "Two tough surgeries and my nerves need a drink in order to calm down."

"Losing my billfold didn't help me either," Dr. Freeland added

"Coming up, doctors," she responded. At fifty-nine, Maisie looked much younger and her brunette beauty hadn't faded. She was warm, vivacious and she loved to talk—a trait that was invaluable in a tavern owner.

In the months she had owned the tavern, which she had named after herself; Maisie had come to know the doctors from the nearby hospital. "Both for you, Dr. Simms?" she asked grinning.

"No. One for each of us. This is our farewell drink. Dr. Freeland and I are soon off to California."

"In that case, I'll have to tabulate your final bill, Dr. Simms. Your bar tab is getting quite high," she added, with a mischievous smile.

Dr. Freeland with his good looks was no match against Timothy Simms when it came to the ladies. Dr. Simms was noted not only for his bedside charm, but for his quick wit. His practice was filled mostly with women and he planned to take his charm to California soon to join a new practice.

"That's exactly what I plan to do—get quite high," Dr. Simms mused. He glanced over at Dr. Freeland, sitting next to him, who appeared to be deep in thought.

"Hey, Jonathan, come out of it. You're miles away." Dr. Simms turned and grasped his friend's shoulder in his hands.

Jonathan looked and with a shrug, he replied, "Lots on my mind."

"Well, let's take our drinks over to a booth and talk about it." Dr. Simms waved Maisie over. "We're heading to a booth. Please bring two more bourbon and waters over. And bring my tab too."

Dr. Freeland took a seat in the booth and looked at his drinking companion thoughtfully. "Tim, I met a remarkable young woman tonight. Her name is Katherine Kincaid and I took a photo of her."

"Hey man, your wife will really like that," Tim said as he leaned over and grinned.

"Nothing romantic going on," Dr. Freeland was quick to reply. "Remember, I mentioned that I lost my wallet earlier. She's the girl in the laundry room who found it. And even though she has one hell of a birthmark along the right side of her face, she had an unwavering spirit. I decided I want to help her. So, I want to give the photo to you so you could send it to your friend, Dr. Reuben Cummings."

"Why?" Dr. Simms looked bewildered.

"You're joining his practice. And he's one of the best plastic surgeons in the country."

"So?"

"So, while you're doing lucrative tummy tucks and breast augmentations, he'll still be doing facial surgeries and laser treatments on birthmarks."

"Right. And, my dear Jonathan, if you would agree to join us you could do very well financially in the practice."

Jonathan glared at the other doctor. "You don't understand, Tim. I am not interested in making a lot of money. Right now, I'm interested in helping this young woman get rid of her birthmark because I believe it's ruining her life. She's stuck in the basement laundry room, while she wants to go to school and study to become a nurse. She returned my wallet and I want to reward her by helping her."

"That's an expensive reward my friend. I think you ought to slow down," Tim suggested.

"No. Helping her would be the right and good thing for us to do. There's a three hour difference in the time between here and California. Let's call Dr. Cummings and see if the three of us can remove this young girl's birthmark."

Tim looked at Jonathan with skepticism.

"Please Tim, I beg of you." Jonathan pleaded earnestly.

Tim thought for a few moments and then nodded. "I have his number in my wallet."

Jonathan released a breath of relief. "I'd like to get started on this project soon." He snapped his fingers. "Give me Cumming's phone number and I'll call him."

"Boy, you are really hopped up over this girl," Tim said

"Right now, I'm going to call Harold Saxton and see if we can get one of his famous grants to do this work," Jonathan said.

"I don't think that calling him this late at night is a good idea.""Nothing ventured. Nothing gained." After dialing the number, he said, "Harold, this is Jonathan Freeland calling. I have a very special problem I want to discuss with you."

"Hell man, do know what time of night it is. I was already in bed and I have an eight o'clock meeting in the morning with the grant board." Harold Saxton's voice sounded a little upset.

"That's what I wanted to talk to you about Harold, a grant. I'd like to meet with you and the board to discuss a special needs grant. I know a young lady who has a terrible birthmark on her face. And I'd like funding to study what effects laser treatments or plastic surgery would have on her. In fact, I'd like for you and the board to meet this young woman before you consider the grant."

"Dr. Freeland, it's very late to discuss this in detail." Harold's voice was now sharp and cross as he snapped, "If you want us to consider the grant, I suggest you stop by the board meeting at eight. Right now, it's past my bed time. Good night."

After he talked on the phone, Jonathan gave Tim the thumbs up.

Jonathan Freeland looked down at the bourbon and water that was sitting in front of him. Without hesitation, he drank it straight down. Then sighing, he looked at Tim. "At least he didn't say no. Maybe I have a good shot at the grant. Now, I've got to get home to my wife."

As they stood up, Maisie walked over. "Oh Dr. Simms, I've got your bar tab ready."

Tim laughed and reached into his pocket for his credit card. "Put it on here and add an extra $20 as a tip for yourself."

"In that case, how about another bourbon and water for each of you?"

Jonathan waved his hand. "I think I've had enough. I'll call you tomorrow Tim and let you know how I made out with Saxton and the grant. I'll plan on calling Dr. Cummings after I find out more."

Outside, Jonathan dashed to his car and climbed in. "Now, where did Katherine Kincaid say she lived?" he asked out loud. Then answered himself. "Oh yes, in a brownstone on the corner of James and 48th street. Even though it's late, I need to visit her and her mother and tell them of my plans."

Dr. Freeland headed to the Kincaid home and stopped in front of the building where Katherine lived. He got out of the car and walked up on the porch.

He rang the doorbell not once but twice. After waiting a few minutes, he knocked several times. Katherine had said she lived with her mother, who also worked in the laundry.

Finally, the inner door to the brownstone opened. Standing behind the locked screen door stood a tall slender woman with graying hair, who appeared to be in her late fifties.

Jonathan took a step closer to the door. "Mrs. Kincaid?"

"Yes, I'm Mrs. Kincaid. And who are you?"

"I'm Dr. Jonathan Freeland, from the hospital." He pulled out his hospital ID badge and flashed it at her. "May I come in? I have something very important I would like to discuss with you and your daughter."

Harriett looked befuddled. "It's very late. Can't this wait until morning when Katherine is awake?"

"No. It's important and I need to discuss this with you both now," he replied in a determined voice.

Harriett took a step backward, somewhat alarmed. "What about my daughter. Is there a problem at the hospital?"

"No. Everything is fine. May I come in? I have something urgent

I wanted to talk to both of you about. It can't wait."Harriett opened the door and ushered him inside. She motioned for him to have a seat on the living room sofa.

Standing directly in front of him, with her hands on her hips, she asked, "Well, what is it?"

"First of all, I want to tell you I just met your daughter earlier this evening. I lost my wallet while in the surgery center. She found it in the laundry and returned it to me."

Fear crept into Harriett's voice. "Was everything in it when you got it back?"

"Of course. The wallet is not what I want to talk to you about."

"Well, what is it then? It's quite late you know." She scowled.

"I realize that." He patted the cushion on the sofa. "Please have a seat beside me and we can talk something over. I'll be brief."

After Harriett reluctantly sat down, Jonathan continued, "Well, here goes. I have a colleague who specializes in laser treatments and plastic surgery. I want to take Katherine to California with me so a couple of doctors can possibly remove that birthmark. And, I'm fairly certain that I can get a grant to cover the cost of her treatments."

Before Harriett could answer, a voice rang out from the doorway. Katherine was standing there in her robe and slippers. "I heard the door bell ring. What's going on Momma?"

"It's Dr. Freeland. Here from the hospital. He wants to talk to both of us."

Katherine stepped inside the living room. "Oh yes, Dr. Freeland", she replied looking at him in astonishment. Nervously, she asked, "Did I just hear you say that you wanted to remove my birthmark?"

"Yes. But first, I'll need to get your mother's permission because you're underage."

Katherine raced over to the sofa, sat down and took her mother's hands in hers. "Did you hear that Momma? Maybe he can remove my birthmark."

Harriett slipped back deeper into the cushions of the sofa. "Yes. I'm not deaf." She frowned and looked at her daughter with deep concern and reservations. "But, I have to think about it. This is so sudden. And Katherine is too young to go off to California with a stranger."

Jonathan stood up and started to pace anxiously, "Mrs. Kincaid, we don't have time to sit and think about this. I plan to go before a board that gives out grants 'for research and projects such as this. And I'm meeting with them at eight in the morning. That's why I'm here so late. There's no sense in pleading Katherine's case if you're not going to give your permission for us to proceed with the treatment."

Harriett replied angrily, "This is all taking place too fast."

Katherine threw her arms around her mother's shoulders. "Please, Mamma, just say yes."

"I'll take care of all the arrangements," Dr. Freeland said. "My wife will be along as a chaperone. And I expect the grant to cover all the expenses."

"You're sure? I don't have any money," Harriett replied.

Katherine slid closer to her mother. "Please, say yes, Momma. Dr. Freeland is a good man."

Dr. Freeland could see that Harriett was now warming to his idea. "I'll have to have some papers signed before I can proceed with the treatment."

"What about Katherine's job at the hospital. Won't she lose that if she goes to California for treatment?" Harriett asked anxiously.

"Don't worry. I'll take care of that. With your approval, I'll present my idea to the grant board this morning. If they give me the go ahead, I'll return later with papers for you to sign."

Harriett sighed and nodded her agreement. "Make it late in the afternoon. Katherine and I go to work about seven at night. Also, how long would my daughter be in California?"

"The procedure will probably take several weeks."

With a quivering voice, Katherine whispered, "I know this was meant to be Momma."

Harriett looked apprehensive. "Maybe God sent you to us, doctor. I just hope you can make my little girl as beautiful in her appearance as she is in her heart."

"My colleagues and I will do our very best. I'll give you more details tomorrow."

He looked at Katherine. "I want you go with me to the board meeting this morning. I think it would be best if they could see how much you need this procedure."

"Whatever you say," Katherine replied.

"I'll pick you up around seven-thirty," Dr. Freeland said. He shook hands with both of the ladies and quietly left.

After he was gone, Katherine started to sob quietly. Harriet came over and hugged her. "Try to get some sleep. I'll call you about seven so you have time to get dressed."

"I love you Momma. Please say a prayer for me. This could change my whole future."

# Chapter 5

"In the kitchen, Dear," Casey Freeland replied after Dr. Freeland entered the front door and called out, "I'm home, Honey."

He walked into the kitchen to find his wife sitting on a bar stool next to the kitchen island, sipping on a hot chocolate and eating a piece of toast. She looked up and said with a faint smile, "You and one of your colleagues stopped for a drink after surgery, I take it?"

Dr. Freeland slipped up behind his wife, kissed her on the cheek and gave her a hard squeeze.

"Easy, boy. I need to breathe," she said motioning for him to have a seat beside her.

"Yes. Dr. Simms and I needed to unwind and talk something over." His eyes narrowed, "I'm so wound up, I hope that I can get to sleep. And I've got to get up early."

"Well, sit down and give me the details. Good news, I hope."

He leaned forward, a serious look on his face. "Darling, I met a girl tonight. Not, just any girl."

"Well, I know it's not your new operating nurse. She's old and..."

He put a soft palm over her mouth and pressed himself against her side. "Please Casey, this is serious."

With a shrug, she responded jovially, "I'm certain I won't be able to sleep either, until I hear your story. So get to the part that'll tell me the reason you're so hyped up."

For the next fifteen minutes, Dr. Jonathan Freeland rambled on about how Katherine Kincaid had come into his life. His wife listened intently and a wave of compassion swept over her when Jonathan told her how the ugly birthmark marred Katherine's almost perfect beauty.

He concluded. "And finally, my Dear, I plan to take this young woman with me to the grant board meeting in the morning. They'll be able to see how desperately this girl needs help and hopefully will give us a financial grant that'll enable us to take her to California for treatment with the specialist that Dr. Simms is planning to work with."

"This sounds like a splendid idea, Jonathan. I'm glad to hear you and Tim are so willing to donate your time and skills to a worthwhile effort. But do you think the grant board will listen to you?" She smiled, trying to mask her uneasiness.

"Well, one of my main selling points to the board is that I'll film and record the whole procedure so it can be recorded in the medical journals. It'll help other doctors to treat cases like this. I'm hoping you'll go along with me to the board meeting. I need all the support I can get. We'll have to get up at six-thirty in the morning, so we'll have time to pick up Katherine and get to the meeting. Hopefully, the board will give us the grant when they see how desperately this young woman needs it in order to lead a normal life and have a real future. Her past is so sad, but yet, she remains very upbeat. And I'm fortunate I got an okay from her mother to proceed with the proposed treatment."

Casey put her arm around her husband's shoulders. "If it's meant to be, then I'm sure you'll get the grant. Is Dr. Simms ready to go along with you on this?"

"Actually, he encouraged me to go for it. I have to fill out the formal papers for the grant request. Then, it's time to head for bed. Want to look fresh in morning. I'll set the alarm," Jonathan replied.

After he was in bed, Jonathan found that thoughts kept racing around in his mind. Finally, he took a sleeping pill so he could get a few hours of sleep.

His wife, on the other hand, had no trouble falling quickly asleep. She felt that faced with Jonathan's determination, the board would have to say yes.

In the morning, they both rose after hearing the alarm. After a fast shower, they dressed and went to the kitchen where they had a quick breakfast of cold cereal and juice. After calling Katherine to tell her they were on the way to her house, they headed out the door.

When they arrived at the Kincaid home, they found Katherine standing at the curb, waiting for them.

Shortly before eight, they entered the conference room where the grant board was meeting.

With his wife and Katherine behind him, Jonathan Freeland walked up to Harold Saxton. "Morning, Mr. Saxton, I'd like you to meet my wife Casey and this is Katherine Kincaid, the young lady I'm requesting the grant for." Jonathan handed Harold the papers he had prepared the precious night for the grant request.

The elderly man's high leathery brow was crisscrossed with a deep pattern that bore witness to his years of enjoying the outdoors. His beaming smile deepened the groves arcing from his nose to the corners of his mouth and beyond. When he smiled his weathered face dropped about ten years.

Harold Saxton shook hands briefly with Casey Freeland. When he turned to Katherine, he suddenly took a quick step backwards. The severity of Katherine's disfigurement on her otherwise beautiful face took him by surprise.

At Harold's urging, Jonathan, Casey and Katherine sat down at a long table in the front of the room. From a side door, the other members of the board entered and took their seats at a dais in the front of the room, facing the table.

Harold Saxton gave each member of the board a copy of the grant request and introduced them. "First, Dr. Freeland, this is Mrs. Smith, Mrs. Roman and Mr. Russo. Together with me, they will hear your case. In a few words, tell us why you are asking for this grant of a half a million dollars."

Dr. Freeland stood. "First, I'd like to introduce my wife, Casey. She is here for moral support."

Casey nodded to the panel.

"Then, I want you to meet Katherine Kincaid," Dr. Freeland motioned for Katherine to stand up. "Katherine is just under eighteen. She currently works at St. Regis Hospital in the laundry room with her mother. Because Katherine is underage, her mother has consented to the treatment for Katherine and has agreed to sign the appropriate legal papers."

He motioned for Katherine to sit down as he continued, "Ms. Kincaid was born with the birthmark you see on her face and has never had any treatment for it because of her financial situation. What I purpose to do is to take her to California, where two specialists and I will introduce new laser surgery to treat the birthmark. Because the proposed treatment is so new, it will be necessary to keep Katherine in the hospital there, where her treatments and daily progress can be monitored and recorded. What I plan to do is to document the entire procedure with photographs and video taken during the course of action. I'll get a medical publication published afterwards so the procedure would be available for other physicians to deal with birthmarks, tattoos and other ugly imperfections or scars."

Harold Saxton and the board reviewed the papers in front of them and they listened intently as Dr. Freeland continued, "I would also use the medical report as a supplement when I address the next plastic surgeons' medical conference. So you see, ladies and gentleman, this grant would not only help Katherine but would advance the future treatment of such afflictions."

When he finished his speech, Dr. Freeland turned to Katherine. "Now, I would like Ms. Kincaid to say a few words. Afterwards, you may question her if you wish."

His introduction of her, jarred Katherine out of her sober thoughts and she stood up hesitantly. "Thank you, Dr. Freeland." She smiled shyly. "I was born with this birthmark and I've been saving my money from working in the laundry. My goal is to attend nursing school and get a degree. Afterwards, I hope to work as a nurse at St. Regis Hospital." A note of sadness entered her voice as she added, "Looking as I do presently, I'm afraid getting a job that involves dealing with the public would not be easy for me."

An elderly woman on the board raised her hand. Her skin which was like crepe paper, betrayed her age. "Katherine, I am Susan Smith and I'm glad to meet you. You seem to be a very upbeat young lady."

Katherine smiled. "I hope and pray that Dr. Freeland can work a miracle for me. My mother has spent years hiding me. She was worried that people would look at me and ridicule me. She has faith that with the removal of my birthmark I might fit in more easily in society. If you decide not to give Dr. Freeland the grant, that won't deter me from my quest to get this birthmark corrected. I will still someday find a means to accomplish my goal. I just don't know when and if it will happen without your help."

Harold stood up. "I think the board has seen and heard enough. At this time, I would like to propose that we approve Dr. Freeland's grant in the amount that he has requested. All those in favor, please raise their hands."

Jonathan held his breath as he waited for an answer. Katherine stared in amazement, when after a few seconds, the hand of every board member shot into the air.

"Well, Dr. Freeland, it looks as if the board is giving you the grant," Harold said. "It will probably take about a month before we have everything in place and can start funneling the money to you."

Jonathan nodded. "That's okay. Yes, Sir, that's okay."

With tears in his eyes, he jumped to his feet, hugged Katherine and his wife and then rushed to each of the board member and vigorously shook their hands.

As they left the conference room, Jonathan turned to his wife and Katherine and said, "I've got to call Dr. Simms and tell him we've got the okay on the project. Then, I'm buying both of you the biggest breakfast ever. And I won't take no for an answer, Katherine."

With a big smile breaking out on her face, Katherine replied, "Thank you. But, I've got to find a phone first. I want to call my mother and give her the good news?"

"Yes, my Dear. Call her at once."

# Chapter 6

Dr. Freeland was delighted the board had approved the grant. The fact it would take a month before the money would be actually available gave him ample time to get the planned procedure formalized. He and Dr. Simms planned to get Dr. Ronald Cunningham, the specialist in California lined up to work with them.

The dates had to be set up so all the three participating doctors in the procedure would be available at the same times. This big adventure was to be documented on both film and in a written journal. Consequently, the doctors had to find a film crew to work with them.

While waiting for her departure for California, Katherine continued to work with her mother in the laundry room.

After three weeks, Dr Freeland received word the grant had been finalized and the funds could be released in segments. Dr. Freeland, his wife and Katherine were excited when the day finally arrived that they could depart. They were scheduled to stay in Dr. Cunningham's spacious four-million-dollar home which was located between Santa Barbara and Los Angeles.

After Dr. Cunningham examined Katherine, he decided the birthmark not only covered the side of her face, but that the mass also was deep into the tissue. Rather than treat it with laser as was originally planned, it was decided to surgically remove the birthmark with an operation and then to use a skin graft from Katherine's thigh to cover the bare spot. This course of action could then be followed with laser treatments if necessary.

Before the procedure could begin, Katherine would undergo a

complete physical examination and several pints of her blood were drawn to keep on hand for the operations.

The first operation took the three doctors over five hours to remove the major portion of the birthmark. It went well but afterwards Katherine was in some pain.

The surgeons waited a week before they undertook the second step. The entire procedures were filmed and Dr. Freeland planned to add the audio explanation later.

Throughout the surgeries, and the time in between them, Katherine remained very positive. To pass the time, she read medical journals. Study and reading during her time in California helped Katherine prepare to enter nursing school. After receiving her nursing degree, she hoped to one day study to become a doctor.

The first laser treatment had left Katherine in minor pain. Dr. Cunningham told her a patient he had recently removed a tattoo from, had said that she never had been in as much agony as when the she had the tattoo taken off.

In spite of her pain after the various treatments, Katherine never complained, but instead, kept her mind focused on the anticipated final result.After the last treatment, Dr. Cunningham put a large bandage on Katherine's face to make sure her face would remain dry and no infection would set in.

After several weeks, two surgeries, two skin grafts and three laser treatments, the doctors were elated to see how well Katherine was now looking and had planned a small celebration for her.

The celebration was interrupted by Dr. Freeland's wife, Casey. "Sorry Dear, I have to fly back to Philadelphia. My sister called and my mother suffered a stroke. She's in the hospital and I need to be there for her."

Dr. Freeland approached the other two doctors who had been working with him. "I think my work here is finished and I must accompany my wife back home."

He thanked Dr. Cunningham for his hospitality and then turned to Katherine. "We need for you to stay an extra week or two. The last skin graft has made the side of your face very tight. So Dr.

Cunningham wants you to try some special creams to loosen the skin. Also he'll have a cosmologist come in to help you learn to apply special make up. When it's time for you to return to Philadelphia the doctor will help you make the arrangements. Here's a credit card to use for your expenses."

"Whatever you think is best," Katherine said. She was startled at this unexpected piece of news and her eyes widened.

"I'd like to thank all of you for making these past weeks the happiest of my life." She held onto Dr. Freeland's hand and seemed reluctant to let go. Tears formed in Dr. Freeland's eyes.

The doctors were very proud of how Katherine now looked. The operations and skin grafts had tremendously improved her appearance. With the help of carefully applied make up, her scars would be barely visible.

While Katherine stayed on in California, residing at Dr. Cunningham's home in-between the treatments, both Dr. Freeland and Casey returned to Philadelphia. Dr. Simms stayed in California where he was going to take over Dr. Cunningham's practice.

For the next six months, Dr. Cunningham planned to work part time in the practice to help Dr. Simms get established. Both Dr. Cunningham and Dr. Simms were disappointed that their friend and colleague, Dr. Freeland, had concluded the California life-style wasn't for him. He had decided to give special lectures on the work the three doctors had done on Katherine's birthmark. Their procedure, which was new to the medical world, would be used in numerous future operations. Additionally, Dr. Freeland knew his wife was reluctant to leave her parents.

When the two doctors decided they had done all they could for Katherine, Dr. Simms helped her arrange a direct flight on the red-eye to Philadelphia and home. At Dr. Freeland's insistence, Dr. Simms had booked a first class seat for Katherine, so she was able to stretch out and sleep comfortably on the flight.

Arriving at the Philadelphia airport at seven in the morning, Katherine went straight to baggage, picked up her luggage, and headed outside the terminal to locate the shuttle bus that would take her home. She knew her mother and Phyllis were awaiting her arrival with great anticipation.

As soon as the shuttle pulled up in front of the apartment, both the ladies ran outside and threw their arms around Katherine and hugged her. Then taking a few steps back, they stared at her with amazement. They could not believe what a transformation had taken place on Katherine's face.

"My God, girl," Harriett exclaimed with elation in her eyes. "You're beautiful."

Phyllis nodded. "The doctors did a fantastic job. You look so much different."

Picking up her luggage, they led Katherine into the apartment where they sat down. Both of the women began throwing questions at Katherine about her time in California. She told them how wonderful staying at Dr. Cunningham's house was and how the treatments had progressed. "Sorry, I didn't call much while I was gone. I wanted to stay focused and to get the operation behind me."

"That's okay. We understood," her mother answered.

"Before I left, I sent Dr. Cunningham a beautiful flower arrangement with a thank you card," Katherine added.

Later, while they were eating lunch, the phone rang.

Harriett jumped up to answer it. "Yes. Yes. She's here. Just a minute."

She handed the phone to Katherine. "It's for you, my angel."

"This is Katherine. Yes, Mrs. Freeland. I got home safely. No problems. And my mother and our friend, Phyllis, are delighted with the results. Yes. I am free tonight. Yes. I'll be there."

When she hung up the phone, Katherine looked at her mother. "You know I'm anxious to spend some time with the two of you, but Mrs. Freeland just invited me to a surprise party tonight for Dr. Freeland. He decided to retire after working at St. Regis for twenty-five years. I told Mrs. Freeland I'd meet her at the front door of the Hotel Mercer at six forty-five."

With a ragged sigh, Phyllis looked at Katherine. "Okay, that settles it. This afternoon, we're going to treat you to a facial and have something done to your hair. Then, we'll stop by Macy's and get you a beautiful dress and accessories."

Harriett clapped her hands in excitement. "All the people at the hospital will be amazed to see your transformation. Yes, my gorgeous daughter, you are ready for the world now. And I really want to show you off. You are pretty enough to be a fashion model."

"Slow down Momma. My next step is to become a nurse," Katherine answered. Then, she turned to Phyllis and gave her a hug. "Your faith in me will never be forgotten. Someday, I'll have the title of 'doctor,' thanks to you."

Phyllis smiled. "For you, my dear Katherine, I believe the sky will be the limit."

# Chapter 7

The Hotel Mercer was the scene of the tribute to Dr. Freeland who was retiring after serving on the staff of St. Regis Hospital.

The dinner started in the elegant ball room at seven. The round tables had black tablecloths and the glistening white china and napkins were the perfect accent. Above, the many crystal chandeliers glistened.

In front of the tables, were a dais, long table, podium and microphone. Seated at the table were the Hospital's President and Chief of Staff, five board members, the mayor, Dr. and Mrs. Freeland, Katherine Kincaid, and two of Dr. Freeland's colleagues

Several minutes were spent on introductions and a speech by the Chief of Staff, Dr. Deland Myers. Next he called up Dr. Freeland's colleagues, who related stories of how great Dr. Freeland was to work with and told a couple of humorous incidents

After the speeches, Dr. Myers announced that a very special young lady had been invited to introduce Dr. Freeland to the audience.

"Miss. Kincaid, would you please come to the podium?"

All eyes were on Katherine as she arose from her seat and walked slowly to the center of the dais. Standing before the attentive audience, Katherine said simply, "I am honored to introduce to you my friend and mentor, Dr. Jonathan Freeland. He helped to change me from a child and a recluse to the young woman you see standing before you. I give you, my dear savior, Dr. Freeland."

Dr. Freeland stared at Katherine in amazement. He had not

seen her since he left California weeks before, and the final results of her transformation were amazing. She was dressed in a short emerald green satin dress that clung to her body like a second skin. Her shoulders were bare except for tiny spaghetti straps that were encrusted with rhinestones. Her flaming red hair was drawn back in an elegant chignon with rhinestone clips holding it in place. Her feet were clad in satin shoes the same color as her dress. Her jewelry was a single strand of rhinestones around her neck and she wore tiny diamond studs in her ears. All of this was a perfect frame for her peaches and cream complexion and her unmarked face. She was not only beautiful, but absolutely stunning.

He walked up to her and sent her a playful grin. As they embraced, he recalled how she had looked when he had first seen her. "You look sensational," he whispered in her ear.

Katherine was almost bubbling with exhilaration. "Thanks to you." She lifted her glowing damp eyes—moist with happiness. She smiled back at him, kissed his cheek and returned to her seat.

Dr. Freeland stood at the podium as Dr. Myers presented him with a plaque. "Jonathan, this plaque honors your twenty-five years of dedicated service to the hospital and the community. Everyone at the hospital will miss you as we send you and your wife, Casey, on your way to the retirement that you so richly deserve. It will be very difficult to find anyone to take your place." Unable to keep the pride from his voice, he added, "Additionally, your name will be on the entrance of the new children's wing of the hospital."

Dr. Freeland briefly thanked him for the honor, then gave a short speech thanking everyone for their friendship and years of help.

After the dinner, Katherine talked briefly with Jonathan and Casey Freeland. She hooked her arm through Jonathan's and stepped closer as she thanked them once again for their many kindnesses. "Now," she said with confidence, "I'm ready to start my life anew."

The next three years passed by quickly for Katherine as she attended nursing school and obtained her certification as a registered nurse.

After graduation, she took a full time position at St. Regis's.

Dr. Freeland had not simply retired as he had earlier planned. After writing several medical journal articles describing Katherine's surgery and recovery he had found a new career. He took his reports and video to medical conventions where he spoke to other doctors about the complicated procedures used to remove Katherine's birthmark. Eventually, his journals were published in a book and he spent months on tour to promote it.

It had now been nine months since Katherine had started working as a registered nurse. She soon became known to her patients as "Nurse K." She rushed around her floor as if she were on wheels—using her time to learn all the aspects of her job.

"Where do you get your energy?" the other nurses would ask as she worked ten hour shifts. Her warm and caring bedside manner made all her patients love her.

"You were meant for this job," everyone would tell her. To this she didn't respond, the point was well taken.

As summer came to an end, Dr. Freeland and his wife returned from a trip to Spain where he had been the central speaker at a world-wide medical convention. They phoned Katherine and invited her to dinner Sunday evening.

She was a little breathless as she walked in their front door. "Sorry I'm late. I just love going to the gym and running on the treadmill on my days off. And then, of course, I had to take time to shower before I came here." She gave them an apologetic smile.

"I'd think you get enough exercise running up and down the halls of the hospital all day," Casey said, putting her arm through Katherine's and leading her to the living room sofa. "They're lucky they don't have to pay you by the mile."

"They couldn't afford her then," Jonathan responded.

"Somehow, the treadmill gives me a chance to unwind," Katherine said as she sat down.

"Well, you look wonderful. In fact, you look more beautiful each time I see you. You must have lots of young men begging you for a date. Please tell us that a Mr. Right has come along."

Katherine laughed. "My dear Casey, romance is on the back burner for now." Then, trying to change the subject, she added, "I hope you took a lot of pictures while you were in Spain." She crossed her legs and leaned forward. "Now that you've returned from your trip, what do you have planned for the future?"

Casey looked over at her husband and said with a suppressed smile, "What we have planned isn't very significant. What's really important is the surprise that Jonathan has planned for you."

Jonathan studied his wife thoughtfully for a moment. "You didn't tell her yet, did you, Casey?"

"No, Dear. It's your big moment."

"You guys are moving to Florida. Right?" Katherine asked.

"Maybe someday. But not now," Jonathan said.

Katherine sat on the edge of her seat. "You guys are killing me. Tell me. Or I'm liable to flip out."

"Maybe we should eat first, Casey," Jonathan teased.

His wife swung her head around, fixing him with a cold glare. "No. Tell her."

Jonathan grinned. "Listen up. I'm about to knock your socks off."

"Yes?" Katherine said in anticipation.

"Starting in September, you're going to the University of Pennsylvania. You're going to change your title from Nurse Kincaid to Doctor Kincaid."

The room was deadly silent as Katherine stared at him in amazement. "No. I can't believe that."

"I know it won't be easy. But hell, you can do it. And now for the really great news. Each year, the hospital gives out a full scholarship to a medical school. And you've gotten it. All you have to do is to say 'yes'."

"Say yes. My God—yes! I mean wow! I can't believe this. Tell me more, please."

"I went to the hospital board that established the medical school scholarships and submitted your name. With your experience and the excellent references you received from everyone you worked with, you won hands down. Monday morning you're scheduled to meet with the board. And look out, young lady, the University of Pennsylvania, here you come. It's no surprise to everyone who knows you that you were destined to obtain great success one day. And well, that day is now," Dr. Freeland said.

Like a torrent of water from an unseen place, feelings of elation swept over Katherine. "Well, I could not be more thrilled. Imagine me going to the University of Pennsylvania to become a doctor. This is beyond my wildest dreams. But, I have so much to learn."

"You probably don't' remember that I graduated from there," Dr. Freeland added. "It's the fourth best school in the nation to turn out doctors. Your nursing career will be on hold of course, while you attend the school, but your nursing background will be of great help to you in your studies. And speaking of studies, you'll have to put in long hours on that."

"Think you can handle it?" Casey asked.

"Can I handle it? I don't want to sound conceited but I'm sure I can." She gazed at Jonathan. "You are such a wonderful man. How can I ever repay you for everything you've done for me?"

"Don't worry about that. Just get that degree. I want you to know becoming a doctor won't be easy Katherine."

"I realize that. But don't worry, I'll make you proud of me."


In the fall, Katherine headed for medical school. Her social life would be non-existent. There would be no time for romance as her hours were filled with classes and studies. And the studies were more difficult than Katherine had anticipated.

She carried a huge load of credit hours as a full time student. She had set her sights on becoming a doctor and the years of study were intense. They were followed by an internship. Katherine had informed the board that gave her the scholarship she hoped to eventually return to St. Regis's Hospital.

By taking classes throughout the summers, Katherine graduated in three years. At her graduation, Jonathan and Casey Freeland sat proudly with Katherine's mother, Harriett and her friend, Phyllis Green, to watch Katherine walk up to receive her medical degree. As Katherine walked up to the stage, Harriet leaned over and whispered to Phyllis, "Isn't this a wonderful moment. And to think I almost abandoned her."

Katherine had finally received the long awaited certificate to hang on the wall of her office—Dr. Katherine Kincaid, Graduate of the University of Pennsylvania Medical School.

Katherine went to work at St. Regis's Hospital as an intern and later as a physician.

A couple of years later, when she was attending a medical conference, a tall and heavily built doctor, who appeared to be in his early seventies, approached her.

"Dr. Kincaid, I'm Dr. Dennis Meeks and I'm a friend of Dr. Freeland." He extended his hand. Katherine recognized the voice—low and raspy, with a smoker's North Jersey accent—perhaps originally from Newark or Jersey City.

Katherine grasped his hand firmly. "Yes. I've often heard the good Dr. Freeland speak of you. In fact, he speaks very highly of you."

The doctor smiled in return. "That's how he talks about you. He said you had a great future in medicine. In fact, he told me to grab you if I could to help me in my practice. My son is studying to be a doctor now, but he won't be ready to join me for some time. I need someone right now to help me with my load of patients. And I was hoping that you would say yes."

Immediately after he said this, Dr. Meeks could see he had tweaked Katherine's interest.

"Send me something with the information and I'll look it over and give you my answer in a week or two. Of course, I'll want to talk the offer over with my mentor, Dr. Freeland."

" Good. Now let's go inside and enjoy the rest of the conference."

# Chapter 8

Katherine talked the situation over with Dr. Freeland, and after thinking about her future, she decided to take the position with Dr. Meeks.

Under the tutorage of Dr. Meeks, Katherine learned how to handle his elderly patients with great care and patience and treat ailments that were abundant in the elderly. Within a year, Katherine had fit in well with the practice and felt that she and Dr. Meeks were a good team. Katherine was Dr. Meek's savior as his days of retiring grew nearer.

In addition to working with Dr. Meeks, Katherine had soon learned to work well with Nurse Anita Fox, Dr. Meek's assistant, who helped him both in the office and with his surgeries. Thanks to lots of referrals from present and past patients, the practice grew with leaps and bounds.

Over the next year, Nurse Fox would often say to Katherine, "You need to start another life, Dr. K.—your personal life. When are you getting married?"

Katherine replied in a deliberately absentminded manner. "With Dr. Meeks spending less time in the office, there isn't much leisure time for me to meet someone." Then she added in reluctant agreement, "But yes, maybe someday if Mister Right comes along, I'll consider it."

One day, Anita bounced into Katherine's office waving two tickets in her hand. "He's here. I've got tickets to a talk and book signing by Dr. Walter A. Grayson. He's a good-looking and well-known doctor and he just might be the right fellow for you. I bought his first book and it was wonderful. He's speaking in the local hospital's auditorium and I got two tickets free. It starts at five and I thought we could both go after work."

Reluctantly, Katherine agreed to accompany Anita to the lecture. Still wearing their white lab coats and name tags, they arrived at the auditorium shortly before five and sat down in the back row.

A short time later, a gentleman walked up to the podium and introduced Dr. Grayson. Dressed in casual dark blue slacks and an open necked shirt, Dr. Grayson stepped up to the podium.

Anita leaned over and whispered in Katherine's ear, "Isn't he dreamy? And I understand he's rich."

Katherine could not help but be impressed by the well-built six foot two blond man, who appeared to be in his thirties.

After his speech and the short question and answer period that followed, he sat at the side of the stage signing his books. With his newly purchased second book under her arm, Anita, with Katherine beside her, walked up to the doctor to ask for his autograph.

"Thank you for purchasing my book, Nurse Fox," he said looking at her name tag. Then he glanced over at Katherine, "And what about you, Dr. Kincaid, would you like a copy? It's only..."

Katherine forced a faint smile. "No thanks. I'll read hers'."

Impressed by the attractive female doctor standing in front of him, Dr. Grayson said, "When I'm done here, you two ladies must join me for supper. And I won't take no for an answer."

"I'm sorry, "Anita replied. "My mother hasn't been feeling well and I promised I'd stop by her house and check on her on my way home. But, I'm certain that Dr. Kincaid would love to join you. I know she doesn't have anything planned for this evening." She turned to Katherine. "Isn't that right, Dr. K.?"

Katherine's face was pink with irritation, astonished that Anita had put her on the spot like this.

Dr. Grayson looked amused as he read the expression on Katherine's face. "Then, it's just the two of us, Dr. Kincaid. I insist that you join me."

Katherine glared at Anita, then resigned herself and nodded in agreement.

"Just supper. Tomorrow, I have a busy schedule. I'll have to stop at my office first. Need to take off my lab coat and put on a jacket."

After saying good bye to Anita, Dr. Grayson led Katherine outside to the parking lot, where his Lexus was parked. He helped her get inside and drove to her office where she ran inside and changed quickly. Then, they drove to a nearby restaurant that Katherine had never eaten at before, but recognized it as being very pricey.

Dr. Grayson escorted Katherine inside and greeted the head waiter who called him by name.

After Dr. Grayson spoke briefly, the waiter picked up a menu saying, "I have a quiet table for the two of you."

They were led to a small intimate table in a secluded corner of the room. The wine the doctor selected was delightful and Katherine soon found herself relaxing. Lobster for two was followed by a decadent chocolate dessert. Throughout the meal, they talked intently and soon learned much about each other.

Dr. Grayson seemed particularly interested in Katherine's career. "What are your long term plans for your medical career?"

After some lengthy and deliberate thought, Katherine answered, "I don't think I have made any long term plans at this time. I'm very content with my position with Dr. Meeks right now."

As the doctor dropped Katherine off at her doorstep, she found herself agreeing to accompany him to the opera the following week where they sat quietly through *Madame Butterfly*. Following the opera, they went to a piano bar where they had a couple of drinks and danced. Little did Katherine realize that Dr. Walter Grayson was trying to sweep her off her feet.

Sitting in her apartment, several weeks later, Dr. Grayson asked Katherine a question that left her dumbfounded. "Katherine, how would you like to leave your job and travel with me? I leave on a four week book tour and I'd like you accompany me. That way we can get to know each other better. Then, we'll fly to Hawaii where I have a fantastic home. I'll show you a life like you've never imagined. You'll be living beyond your wildest dreams."

Katherine's mouth fell open in shock. She stared at him, speechless, as he continued, "We'll travel first class and see the world."

He was talking extremely fast. "Please join me. It's time for you to stop working so hard. And I need you in my life. Yes, I need you very much."

"And when would we leave for this adventure?" Katherine asked after several moments. Her tone was skeptical.

"This Saturday. Please say yes." He reached into his pocket. "And I have a gift for you." He handed her a small box. "And for you my Dear, it's just the beginning of all the lavish gifts that I intend to shower on you."

Katherine opened the box and pulled out a black velvet case. Opening it, she found a diamond studded Rolex watch

"First of all, I can't accept this." She grimaced and shook her head. "And secondly, I really don't know you. We've only been seeing each other for a few weeks."

He growled at her through clenched teeth. "What's to know? We can learn about each other when we live together for the next few months. I'm your knight in shining armor and I want to whisk you away."

Katherine shook her head firmly. The whole thing was getting out of hand and her stomach was tight with nerves. "Sorry, Walter you're moving just a little too fast for an old fashioned girl like me."

He jumped to his feet, his face red with irritation. "You're a fool to pass up an opportunity like this. You could live with me and enjoy a carefree life. You would have a beautiful home, expensive clothes, fine food and extensive travel instead of the drab life of a doctor. Yes, Katherine, you are a fool."

"That's your opinion. Not mine. I love my work." Her voice was thick with steadfastness.

Dr. Walter Grayson abruptly left the apartment. He was not used to anyone turning him down and Katherine had made it clear she was not inclined to accompany him on his intended path.

A few days passed and on Saturday morning when Katherine

was on call, her phone rang incessantly.

"I need you at the hospital right away, Dr. Kincaid," Dr. Meeks said. "One of our regular patients was admitted this morning, with a kidney stone and she won't be able to pass it. She insists that she wants you at her side so I want you to give me a hand when I do the surgery."

"Say no more. I'm on my way."

By ten that morning, Dr. Meeks and Dr. Kincaid were prepped. Dressed in surgery garments, a nurse approached them. "Good morning, I'm Alicia Patten and I'll be assisting you."

"We were expecting Nurse Fox to join us. I left a message on her machine," Dr. Meeks said.

The nurse smiled, "Oh, she called the hospital to say she wasn't available. She also said to tell you both that she is quitting her job. She's leaving on an extensive trip with a Dr. Walter Grayson."

Both doctors just stared at each other. Katherine shrugged her shoulders, amused at the irony. "Well, I hope she'll be happy. She's hitched herself to a rocket. And I'm glad that I'm not riding on it."

# Chapter 9

As time went by, Dr. Meeks and Katherine developed a close working and personal relationship.

Occasionally, Dr. Meeks would tease her. "Because all of the male patients are constantly flirting with you, I think I should buy you a ring and have you wear it on your left hand. That way they'll think that you're engaged and stop."

"No," Katherine replied. She dismissed the subject with the wave of her hand and a smile. "I love all of my elderly admirers. It's good for my ego."

After a couple of years, Dr. Meek's son graduated from medical school, did his internship and then joined the practice. In his thirties, Gary Meeks was of medium height, with sandy blond hair and had a stocky built with broad shoulders. Katherine discovered later the broad shoulders were probably from swinging a golf club all the time.

His joining the practice did not turn it into "Three is Company" and often he and his father disagreed on how to run the business. The younger Dr. Meeks favored newer and more modern methods of practicing medicine while his father was set in his old school ways. Soon the elderly Dr. Meeks decided to make plans for retirement. He and his wife wanted to head to Florida and warmer weather.

Working together with Dr. Gary, as the patients called him, Katherine soon learned his first love hadn't been to become a doctor. Rather, his dream had been to hit the big time as a pro golfer. He had attended Stanford University, where he excelled on the golf team. But his game wasn't that of a pro, so he continued with his medical education.

The work load for Katherine kept increasing as both father and son was spending less and less time at the office. On the weekends, Dr. Gary Meeks would spend his time playing in amateur golf championships while his father was staying for weeks at a time in his newly acquired condo in Naples, Florida.

Because of the absence of the two doctors, Katherine was forced to work long hours. In some cases, she had to refer some of the patients to other doctors. And the many hours were starting to take their toll on her.

After Katherine finished with a patient on Friday afternoon, the nurse said, "You only have one patient left to see, a Mr. Clark. And, if you don't mind, Dr. Kincaid, I'd like to leave now. My father is under the weather."

"Sure. Go. See you Monday. Show Mr. Clark in and then you can leave."

As she finished with Mr. Clark, Katherine said, "By the way, Mr. Clark, not only do you need to lose ten pounds, but you've got to quit smoking." She knew he had been actively avoiding both issues.

After he left her office, Katherine cleaned off her desk and turned to hang her lab coat on the nearby coat rack when she heard a voice call out from the reception area, "Hello. Hello. Anyone here?"

She rushed out of her office to see who had entered. Standing in front of her, with his arms casually folded over the top of the reception desk, was a very handsome man, who appeared to be in his early thirties. He stood over six feet tall and had black hair which was prematurely graying slightly at the temples. His eyes were a piercingly sharp exotic shade of gray. Wearing a brown corduroy jacket over tan slacks, he appeared to be a well-dressed and distinguished business man. Katherine thought with his strong profile and good looks, he could have been a male model.

"Hi, I'm Dr. Kincaid. Can I help you?"

"Good afternoon. I'm Mark Keller."

She took a step toward him and added forcefully, "If you're selling anything, you'll need to come back on Monday. Dr. Meeks does all the buying for the office and he's out of town right now. Just leave your card, and we'll get in touch with you."

A broad grin broke across his face. "I'm not here to sell anything. I should have introduced myself. I'm Dr. Mark Keller. My office is nearby and the past couple of weeks, your receptionist has referred some of your patients to me."

"Oh, I was simply overwhelmed. Is there a problem?" With his dark eyes and hair and a hint of a shadowed jaw, he didn't look like the typical image that Katherine had of a doctor.

"Not really." He pulled several pieces of paper out of the briefcase which was sitting at his feet. "I have releases from the patients that the receptionist referred to me and I need their medical records."

"Didn't my nurse send them to you?"

"No. Apparently not."

"Well. We've been swamped. It's late, but give me the list and I'll come in tomorrow, and fax them to you."

Dr. Keller studied his papers, and then shrugged. "Thanks. I'd appreciate that. I think I know why you've been so busy lately," he added softly. "It's all over the sport pages that young Dr. Meeks is two strokes off the lead in the golf tournament he's been playing in this past week."

"Now you know why I'm sending you patients. I'm afraid that by next month, this practice will be closing down," Katherine told him. "The elder Dr. Meeks is retiring and his son seems to be concentrating on his golf game."

Dr. Keller took a step forward. "Listen, how about joining me for supper if you haven't made any other plans for this evening. I hate to eat alone and I might have a solution to your problems and maybe you could help me with mine in return."

Katherine thought for a few minutes and then agreed to accompany the doctor to supper.

As they sat in a small family restaurant, Dr. Keller asked, "May I order for the two of us?"

"Thank you Dr. Keller."

"Please call me Mark. And I'll call you Kate."

"People usually call me Katherine." Then she murmured gently,

"But, I think I'd like you to call me Kate."

Mark ordered two tossed salads with Italian dressing and the homemade lasagna for Kate.

"As for me, I'll have mashed potatoes and the country fried steak."

"You're from the South, I assume, from your slight accent?" Kate asked.

"Yes. From North Carolina." His eyes widened with surprise. "I didn't think I had an accent anymore."

"Well. Shut my mouth," Kate replied laughingly as a cell phone rang loudly.

"That's your phone, Dr. Kate. I turned mine to vibrate."

"Please excuse me," Kate said, as she answered the call. "Yes. Yes. I understand. I'll call you on Monday. Right now, I'm having supper with Dr. Keller. Yes, I understand."

After the conversation, she turned off the phone and placed it back in her purse. "That was Dr. Walter Meeks. He and his wife are moving to Florida permanently. And the younger Dr. Meeks is planning to leave the practice to pursue his dream of being a professional golfer. I guess his next step is to get his pro card. The older Dr. Meeks wants me to close down his practice and sell his equipment." Forcing cheerfulness, she added softy, "And, he would like for you to take his patients, Dr. Keller, if you could."

He clamped his jaw shut. "I'm not sure if that fits into my plans right now. But, let's discuss that later. First, let's eat our salads and I'd like to enjoy my meal. I need to take the time to catch my breath."

With just casual conversation, both finished their dinners.

As she sat back in her chair, enjoying a coffee, Kate said, "My head is still spinning."

"Me too," Mark added. "But the call you got just now from Dr. Meeks didn't seem to surprise you, did it, Kate?"

"No. As I told you before, I expected them to close the practice. But, I'm afraid it might take a few weeks to relocate all the patients. Then, I'll need to find another place to work."

"I just might have a solution to your dilemma," Mark answered.

In the next few months, it was the team of Drs. Keller and Kincaid that took over Dr. Meek's practice. Dr. Keller had added an expansion to his office suites and Kate and Nurse Rodriguez moved in.

Soon, all of Philadelphia would know the new medical team of Keller and Kincaid. As they worked side by side daily and regularly attended social events together, they became very fond of each other.

One Friday afternoon, Mark said to Kate, "Meet me in the office tomorrow morning. I want to rearrange our work schedules. It's a good time for us to start slowing down so bring your workout clothes. I've got your day planned."

"Yes, Doctor, I'll be on time," Kate said fondly.

The next morning, Philadelphia showed signs of the approaching fall weather. The air was cool and crisp and the leaves were just starting to change colors. Once they were seated at Mark's desk, he made out a new schedule for the upcoming months.

"I think we should plan on staying closed on Fridays. This will give us a three day week-end to enjoy ourselves."

Kate nodded in agreement.

"Now, it's time for me to get really serious." He looked intently at Kate. "You know, we've made a wonderful team in our medical practice. I think I'd like to team up with you permanently in our private lives. Well, hell, Kate, what would you think of marrying me?"

Kate leaned back in her chair, her heart pounding. She looked completely stunned as he continued. "Maybe, I'm moving too fast, but from the first time I saw you, I had the idea that you might be the girl for me."

Kate did not move or make a sound. After thinking for several minutes, she reached forward and grabbed Mark's hands. "Yes. Yes. I've told everyone I was waiting for the right guy to come along. And I think you're the one."

Mark jumped to his feet and threw his hands into the air. "Thank you, God."

He reached into the pocket of his warm up suit and pulled out a small box. "I got this ring weeks ago. I was just waiting for the right time to ask you."

He knelt at Kate's feet and slipped the ring on her finger. "Kate, I'll be good to you. I promise."

He reached over and kissed her long and tenderly. "I love you so much."

Since she had grown up without much tenderness, his heartfelt kindness really touched her. She whispered, "Mark, I'll make you a good wife. I promise."

"I know that," he whispered back. "This is October, so let's plan on a January wedding. There's a lot to do before then. I think we should both give up our apartments and buy a house. Have you ever owned a house, Kate?"

"No," she answered, shivering with excitement.

"Let's look for a real estate agent. Lady, hang onto your hat. The team of Keller and Keller is about to take off. Do like the sound of that?"

"That sounds good for our personal life, but professionally I would like to keep it Keller and Kincaid."

He grinned. "That's okay with me."

# Chapter 10

Some women longed for a Prince Charming, but all Katherine Kincaid wanted was Dr. Keller. She had decided he was indeed the right man for her.

As their practice together grew, they decided to move it to the new medical building, which had room for both doctors, two nurses and a receptionist. Their next planned venture was to get married and spend a ten day honeymoon in London and Paris.

The wedding took place in the local cathedral, all of their friends and relatives attended.

Mark thought Katherine was the most beautiful bride he had ever seen as she walked down the long aisle in an ivory colored satin ball gown with pearls and crystal beads sprinkled all over the bodice. The cathedral length train was edged with pearls and crystal beads.

Mark's father escorted Katherine down the aisle. Mark's former college roommate was his best man and Mark's sister served as Maid of Honor for Katherine. Katherine's only regret was that her mother and Phyllis had not lived long enough to see her happily married.

Following the wedding which took place in the late afternoon, a sit-down dinner was held for approximately one hundred guests at the near-by country club.

After the honeymoon, they returned to Mark's three bedroom, two bath condo in a gated community and tried to resume their normal everyday lives. Katherine had given up her apartment and they started to look for the perfect house.

Still keeping their respective names of Dr. Kincaid and Dr. Keller, they soon worked out the kinks in their work schedules and managed to adapt to a four day schedule.


After a year of marriage, Katherine blessed her husband with twins, a boy and a girl, who they named Debra and Donald.

During the next twelve years, the closely knit family did everything together. Both of the children attended private pre-schools and elementary schools.

As he grew older, Donald closely resembled his father in appearance, tall and dark-haired. Debra was the spitting image of Katherine with her flowing red hair.

In high school, Debra attended an all-girls school while Donald went to an all-boys school. Now, separated for the first time, the twins still managed to remain very close.

They both graduated with high honors. After their graduations, they took their parents by surprise with their planned futures. While both had said they wanted to attend college eventually, they decided to join the Peace Corps first. They had been accepted and given their first assignment—going to India to work.

"We'll be building homes and working with the poor and sick," Donald said with eagerness.

"Yes. And, we hope you can take some time off from your practice to join us and work at the local hospital there," Debra added, "Don and I are definitely going to work in India and we'd love to have you join us. Then, in a year or so, we'll return to the States go to college."

Katherine and Mark just stared in amazement at their children, stunned at their announcement.

Finally, Don took his mother's hands in his. "Just think about it, Mom."

After deliberating for some time over the suggestion, Mark and Katherine decided to take time off from their lucrative practice and join their youngsters in helping the poor. They hired two doctors to take over while they were gone.

After making a phone call to the hospital in Calcutta, they were notified they would be welcomed with open arms. They were informed they would need passports, shots and a letter indicating they were in perfect health before they could work with the sick in India.

Several weeks later, they joined Don and Debra on a privately chartered plane. Because the plane was loaded with supplies, there was only room for six passengers.

Once they landed in Calcutta, Don and Debra headed for the Peace Corps headquarters while their parents took a taxi to the small hospital where they had been accepted to work. It was a few miles outside of Calcutta. There, they met Dr. Ed Ragan who was director of the facility.

"Good afternoon, Dr. Keller and Dr. Kincaid," he said, fixing his attention on the newly arrived couple. "Boy am I glad to see you," he said warmly as he shook their hands. "I have accommodations for you in a hotel just across the street from the hospital. I'll have a boy take you there. Ask for Aruna and she'll take care of you. She runs the place and is expecting you. We'll plan on having you eat all of your meals in the restaurant at the hotel."

Mark nodded, his face wet with perspiration from the unaccustomed heat. "That sounds great. We could use some time to freshen up."

Dr. Ragan continued, forcing his attention to the dire situation at hand, "See you tomorrow morning at eight. A shipment of flu shots came in the plane you arrived on. So, we expect a big line up for that. You'll be giving out the flu shots for the rest of the week."

"See you early tomorrow," Katherine called out, her face flushed, as she and her husband departed.

For the next three months, the two doctors worked eight to ten hour shifts daily. The line of patients seemed endless. Additionally, Katherine made a few house calls to those who could not get into the hospital.

Both doctors felt like they were making slow progress trying to keep up with the endless problems that confronted them. As the patients made repeat visits to the hospital clinic, they soon came to call Katherine, "Dr. K." Her warm and caring manner made all the patients love her.

A year later, the Keller children, Don and Debra, decided to return to the States and enter college. Both being in the top of their class upon graduation, they had received notification they had received full scholarships to Temple University and felt they could not turn the opportunity down. The only question that confronted the family now was whether Katherine and Mark should return to the States and resume their practice.

After endless nights of long deliberation, Mark and Katherine decided to stay on in Calcutta and work at the hospital. They knew that their practice at home was in good hands with the young doctors that had taken over and felt no need to immediately return to Philadelphia. They realized they were needed more in India and had come to love the gentle people. They decided to sell their home in Philadelphia to the nice young couple who had been renting it.

Time passed quickly and Mark and Katherine had been in India for over four years. Their children were ready to graduate from Temple University and had lined up jobs after graduation.

Don found an up and coming engineering firm that offered him a fine position and Debra went to work for the FBI in Washington in their forensics department.

Mark and Katherine made a brief visit to the States to attend their children's graduations.

"Boy, are we lucky to have such wonderful children," Katherine said proudly to her husband as they watched their children receive their degrees.

"Yes. They have your beauty and my brains," Mark replied, laughing.

After the ceremony, Don approached his mother, "I wish you and Dad would stay in the States and come live near us. I'm renting a three bedroom home, just outside of Philadelphia, with an attached in-law suite. It would be perfect for the two of you when you retire. And, you might decide to find a winter home in Florida or Arizona."

"Retiring is not in our plans now. Your mother and I have decided to return to India to work and live," Mark stated firmly.

Shortly thereafter, Mark and Katherine returned to the place they had come to love, Calcutta. They wanted to dedicate their lives to serving the poor and the sick. They had fallen in love with the people and their simple way of life. But, most of all, they were a dynamic team—still committed to and in love with each other.

Previously, they had both sought happiness with the material things of life; but now they realized that those things weren't important to them anymore.

"As long as we're together," Kate said, "that's what's most important."

Working long hours at the hospital, they went to bed at night, totally exhausted. However, nothing seemed to shatter or crack the firm bond that had developed between them.

They would hold hands and reminisce about their past lives. Sitting together and looking at the photo scrapbook which was filled with pictures of Katherine before and after her surgery, Mark could not believe the hideous birthmark that had scarred his wife earlier. "I wish we had more pictures of you growing up," he told her.

"I didn't have the nicest of childhoods and my mother took very few photos of me," she responded, sadly. "But, that doesn't matter. The future is what's most important."

"Well, you're beautiful now—both inside and out," Mark said, giving her a hug.

"We should plan to visit the kids in the States soon," Katherine said. "And, maybe, sooner than you think, Mark. Today's letter from Don seems to suggest that both he and Debra have found someone special. I know it's a long flight but we are so blessed with having those two wonderful children. And who knows, maybe, in a few years, we'll be grandparents."

# Chapter 11

Following graduation, Debra and Donald remained very close. After a couple of years, Donald's engineering firm offered him the opportunity to transfer to the branch in Orlando, Florida. Jumping at the opportunity to move to a warmer climate, he quickly left his apartment in Philadelphia and moved on.

Working at his new job, Donald struck up a friendship with a co-worker, Connie Myers. They soon discovered they had a lot in common. Both were well educated, athletic and easy going. The six month romance ended with marriage and a weekend honeymoon.

A year later, Debra married Sam Jordan, a Philadelphia lawyer, and later gave birth to a little girl. After a month's leave of absence for the birth of her child, Debra returned to work.

In the meantime, Mark and Katherine continued their work in India, returning to the States every three years for a brief period of time to visit their family.

The years of long hard work and endless hours, finally took their toll on Mark and left him in a weakened condition. When he was stricken with malaria, he did not have the strength to fight it off and soon passed away. The local townspeople and his fellow workers at the hospital were devastated. But no one more so than Katherine. She did not know how she would go on without her soul mate. Where had all the years gone, Katherine asked herself.

Debra and Donald and their spouses flew to India and helped Katherine find a small nearby cemetery in which to bury her loving husband of almost thirty five years. She also bought the plot next to Mark's and told the children this was to be her final resting place.

"Sorry we can't stay longer," Donald told his mother. "As it is, I'm lucky that the firm gave me time off to come here. But, I do have some exciting news. Connie and I are both moving with our jobs. I'm getting transferred from Orlando to Naples, Florida. My company is opening a new office there and they would like for me to get it rolling."

Debra spoke up. "The FBI is going to send me to the Tampa office. I'll be training other people and will eventually be assigned there permanently. So, Don and I will only be miles apart. Sam and I already located an apartment we can rent from month to month for the time being. And maybe, we'll look for a beach home eventually."

"Connie and I plan to buy a house near the Gulf with plenty of room for you, Mom," Don added. "You've worked long enough and now it's time for you to sit in a beach chair and retire. That way, we can all be together."

Katherine stared at her two children for a few moments, before taking their hands. "I'm sorry kids, but my work here isn't done yet. I love the two of you very much and I envy your great plans, but I've got to stay here. This is where my destiny is."

Her eyes filled with tears as she continued, "I want to remain here and carry on the work your father and I started. Retirement is for old people and I'm not old yet. I still have a lot to work to accomplish. I'll miss you and your families, but I've got to stay here. Now, give me a hug and a kiss. And please, don't stop calling. It means so much to me to hear from you regularly."

The following day, Don and Debra and their spouses were on a plane headed back to the States, while Katherine remained in Calcutta. While she was unhappy knowing she would only see her children every couple of years, Katherine was content to remain in India, knowing her work would probably never be completely finished.

Working on her feet all day at the hospital, soon began to take its toll on Katherine's aging body. Even though she tried to reduce her long hours, it was almost impossible since the need around her was so great.

At four-thirty in the afternoon, she could feel herself starting to become exhausted. The staff tried to talk her into leaving early and she would say, with an effort, "I'll try." But she never did. She had tried to recruit new doctors and nurses but it was always a struggle to find people who were willing to move to India, and the locally trained people were scarce.

One evening, as she started to leave the hospital, Katherine was approached outside by a tall slender young man, who appeared to be in his late teens. He swallowed uncomfortably. "Good afternoon Dr. K, I'm Pari. I need to ask two favors of you. My mother is very sick. She is at home and I couldn't find anyone to help me bring her to hospital. I was hoping you could come to my home and see her. It's only a short distance from here." He looked pleadingly at her with tears in his eyes.

His request went straight to Katherine's heart. "What's wrong with her?"

"I don't know. That's why I wanted you to examine her." His words came across to her in slow, painfully deliberate tones.

"Give me a moment while I grab my bag." Katherine sighed and shrugged her shoulders. Somehow, she could not bring herself to ignore his plea.

She left the young man standing in the lobby while she went to her office and grabbed her medical bag. Returning to the lobby, she said to Pari, "Lead the way."

As they walked to his house, Katherine glanced over at the young man and forced herself to ask, "You said that you wanted two favors. What is the second one?"

"Yes, Missus. I want to become a nurse. I heard you're always looking for assistance." His eyes narrowed and he pleaded, "Can you tell me how I can become a nurse?"

Katherine smiled at him. "Of course I'll help you. We can always use all the help we can get at the hospital. However, it takes a lot of work and study to become a qualified nurse."

He took a step closer to her and replied confidentially, "Oh, I'm young and strong. And I'm smart too."

Katherine flashed him a broad smile. "Yes. I can see you are."

"It's not far from here," Pari said.

He stopped in front of a poor and humble, but tidy hovel. "Here we are. This is where I live with my mother, Chahna, and my sister, Sachi."

Katherine followed Pari inside and he led her into a back room where an elderly woman with thin, graying hair lay curled up in a fetal position upon a small cot. She had a ragged, but clean blanket covering her.

"Momma, I brought the doctor." Pari introduced his mother to Katherine as Dr. K. from the hospital. After examining Chahna, Katherine diagnosed her condition and said she would have some medicine sent from the hospital for her. "I think you have a very bad stomach virus," she calmly told the woman.

Looking up at her son, Katherine added, "I need to start your mother on an antibiotic right away. These pills should help the pain too. I think she will be better by morning. Just follow the directions on the bottle, Pari," she instructed as she reached into her bag and pulled out a bottle. "These pills will ease her pain and the meds tomorrow will cure the virus."

As she turned to leave the house, she looked at him. "You said that you had a sister? I'd like to meet her."

"She is very shy, but I will get her from her room." He walked to the back of the house and returned to the main room, leading a small young girl who seemed to be reluctantly following him.

"This is Sachi. She's eight," he said gently.

With her scarf drawn across her face, Sachi came slowly forward to where Katherine was standing.

"Don't look at me," Sachi whimpered.

Filled with pity, Katherine could see that Sachi was hiding her face behind the scarf. She knew just how the child felt. She gently drew her closer and slowly removed the scarf from the child's face. A small birthmark was beneath her right eye.

Sachi shrank back and tears started to roll down her cheeks.

Dr. K. gently put her hands on either side of the little girl's face. "Oh, little one. No need to be so sad. Your mark is not so bad. Tomorrow, you come to the hospital with your brother. I have some creams and powders that you can use to cover it. When we get it concealed, it will hardly be noticeable."

Katherine knelt down next to the girl and turned the right side of her own face toward Sachi. "I used to have a mark on my face too. I don't have the equipment or the knowledge to remove your mark. But, it's not as bad as the one that I had. After you use the creams I give you, it will be hardly visible. Now, wipe your tears and give me a big smile."

Sachi reached up, grabbed Katherine's hands in hers and kissed them. "Thank you. Thank you. You are so good." Slowly her face started to light up with a bright smile.

"Now, that's the smile I've been looking for," Katherine said as she stood up and gave the children a hug before she turned to leave.

Outside, she said to Pari, "When you come to the hospital tomorrow with your sister, I'll give you the creams for her and the instructions on how to use them. Also, I'll give you instructions on how you can become a nurse."

In the following month, Katherine and Pari would become great friends. In the late evenings, when she wasn't working, Katherine invited Pari to her home, where she would assist him in his studies.

As for Sachi, the creams that concealed the birthmark on her face seemed to change her feelings toward life in general.

When Katherine showed Sachi pictures of how she used to look before she had her birthmark removed, Sachi said, "Didn't looking that ugly just make you want to die?"

Katherine shook her head. "At first, I was very sad about it. But, later I learned to live with my appearance and finally, it just made me stronger and stronger. I was determined to get rid of the birthmark someday. And finally, I found some wonderful doctors who helped me do just that. I learned you must be your own person, no matter what obstacles life puts in your path."

Sachi listened solemnly as Katherine continued, "You have to help Pari and your mother around the house. And you have to make sure that you go to school faithfully and study, yes—study and read a lot. Your brother is planning to become a nurse. Why not you?"

The constant words of encouragement from Katherine helped both Pari and Sachi get a new outlook on life.

On Saturdays, Katherine made a point of inviting many of the local children to the hospital, where she would teach them first aide so they could assist their family members if they needed help. Within a month, over a hundred children attended Katherine's classes.

# Chapter 12

Many of Katherine's old acquaintances wondered why she chose to remain in Calcutta, now living alone. Somehow, living in Florida, with her children, sleeping until noon and playing with the grandchildren who had come along in the last few years was not for Dr. K. A life of leisure was not meant for her.

Rather, as a way to thank the dear Lord for all the goodness he had bestowed on her in life, Katherine decided to continue to dedicate her life to the poor. In her earlier years, the good Lord had sent a doctor to remove her hideous birthmark and thereafter she had used her beautiful face and smile to bring comfort to others.

Then, he had given her the means and talent to become a top rated doctor. And finally, he had given her the love of her life—Mark Keller and their two beautiful children and grandchildren. Yes, she had much to be grateful for. Helping the needy was payback and then some. It had become her top priority.

While her beautiful red hair had turned to silver and her body was slowing down, she still managed to work three or four days a week caring for others.

On a Saturday afternoon, Katherine heard a knock on the door of her office. She stood up, opened it and found a tall, stately middle-aged man standing in front of her. "Dr. Kincaid, I am Harry Sloan from the Philadelphia Enquirer."

"Yes..?" She asked in one long drawn-out syllable.

"You are the famous Dr. K as the people call you?"

Her eyebrows lifted in a what-is-this kind of gesture. "Yes. That I am," Katherine replied, laughingly. "Please come in. And what brings you all the way here from Philadelphia, Mr. Sloan? But before you tell me, I want to invite you to sit down and have tea with me. I was just about to partake of high tea. When my husband and I were in London, we were introduced to it."

She motioned for him to have a seat next to her on the sofa that lined the wall on one side of the office. On the table in front of them, were an old silver tea service and a tier tray of sandwiches and biscuits.

"You're in for a real treat. Here, have some cucumber sandwiches and raspberry scones." She poured Sloan a cup of tea and handed him the cream and the tray piled high with the sandwiches and scones.

He took several sandwiches, put them on his plate and nibbled on them as he drank his tea. "Wow. What a delight this is."

After finishing his sandwiches, he selected a couple of the scones. When he was finished, he leaned back in his chair. "Thank you for the tea. Now, Dr. Kincaid, I wish to discuss the reason for my visit. I want to write a three part story of your life for my paper."

Katherine leaned forward and asked skeptically, "Why?"

"You've been selected by ABC News as their Person of the Week for your wonderful work in Calcutta."

She looked surprised and cut him off by holding up a hand. "They know about me?"

"Indeed, Dr. Kincaid."

A chuckle sounded deep in her throat. "While that is very kind, I don't think I've earned such a title."

"Be that as it may. But, before we discuss my plan, I have someone important I want you to meet, doctor," he said enthusiastically.

"Well, Mr. Sloan, I was planning to attend five p.m. mass at nearby St. Michaels Church."

"That's great for the person I want you to meet is scheduled to be at the church for the mass. Why don't we both head over there?"

"Why the great mystery about this person?" Katherine demanded to know, an incredulous frown wrinkling her forehead.

"Just trust me. I have a car outside."

"Well. Okay. If you insist, I'll accompany you," she replied. "Give me a moment. I need to freshen up. Why don't you have another cup of tea while I get my things?"

She stood up and left the room as Sloan poured himself another cup.

"Okay. I'm ready now," Katherine said when she returned.

"Good. Let's go," Sloan said, jumping to his feet.

Later, the car pulled up to the church and they exited. Taking Katherine by the arm, Sloan escorted her inside. The church was dimly lit and only half full.

As they proceeded down the aisle, Katherine could see a small group of children sitting on the steps of the altar. In the midst of them, was a very small old lady dressed in a white habit, with a blue and white veil covering her head. Katherine's eyes strained to get a good look at the woman as they walked up.

"Why it's Mother Teresa," Katherine whispered, as she dropped to her knees in front of the saintly lady.

Mother Teresa looked directly into Katherine's eyes. "Welcome, my child."

"Mother Teresa, is it really you?" Katherine asked in awe.

"Yes. And you are Dr. K. I saw a story about you on the news and Mr. Sloan said he would try to bring you here to meet me." She eased back and sat up taller. "Everyone knows the wonderful work you and your husband have done for our country in the years you have been here. So many years."

Mother Teresa's words went straight to Katherine's heart and she cherished them. "Thank you dear Mother," Katherine whispered humbly as she took the nun's hands in hers and kissed them.

Mother Teresa looked down at Katherine and said with a gentle smile, "I have heard the story of your life and how you overcame much adversity as a child. You are such a courageous woman. And India will be forever grateful to you and your husband for your work here."

"Thank you Mother, but it is I who am grateful for the opportunity to serve that was given to me. Since I arrived in this county many years ago, Mother, I have fallen in love with these wonderful people,"

Katherine replied humbly.

"Bless you my child. Your reward will be great in Heaven for all you have done."

Katherine held Mother Teresa's hands warmly. "It's so wonderful to meet you. You have been my inspiration for years."

Katherine knew Mother Teresa of Calcutta had been born Agnes Bonxha Bojaxhiu in Albania in 1910. Her father died when she was only eight years old, and her mother, a devoutly religious woman opened an embroidery and cloth business to support the family.

After spending her adolescence deeply involved in parish activities, Agnes left home in 1928 and entered a convent in Dublin Ireland. There, she was admitted as a postulant and received the name of Teresa, after her patroness, St. Therese of Kisieux.

She was sent to the Loreto order in India in 1929. There, she joined the Loreto novitiate and made her profession as a Loreto nun in 1937. Later, she taught in the medium school there.

In 1946, on a train journey from Calcutta to Darjelling, Mother Teresa received what she termed the "call within a call" which led to the rise of the Missionaries of Charity family. She would labor at salvation and sanctification of the poorest of the poor. In 1950, the Missionaries of Charity was officially erected as a religious institute for the Archdiocese of Calcutta.

Throughout the 1950s and early, 1960s Mother Teresa expanded her work throughout India and then throughout the world. She was known for her endless work on behalf of the poor and disaster-stricken.

Mother Teresa led Katherine to the door. Outside, Sloan took several pictures of the ladies and the children who had gathered around them.

As she turned to get into her taxi, Mother Teresa said, "There is a new hospital being dedicated for the poor about a hundred miles from here and I promised to be there, so I will leave you now. God bless you my child and I hope you will pray for me."

After Mother Teresa left, Sloan turned to Katherine. "I believe you liked her."

"Like her? I loved her," Katherine said passionately. "She's a saintly woman. She is even more wonderful than I expected. Thank you for giving me the opportunity to meet her. What an honor this has been. Now, I must get back inside for the mass."

Sloan shook her hand. "I'll send you a copy of my story and some of the photos."

"One favor, Mr. Sloan, tell whoever will listen that we need food, medicines and help with our work here."

"Then, why not return with me? You can tell your story in person and ask for assistance."

Katherine shook her head. "No. My work here is not finished. I must remain here, where I'm desperately needed."


In the months that followed, Katherine's health worsened. She had received a copy of the article and the pictures Harry Sloan had written for the Philadelphia Enquirer. The story about Dr. K had touched a countless number of people in the U.S. Several collections were taken up and sent to India to purchase medicines and foods. But even this was just a drop in the bucket compared to the need.

A large framed picture of Katherine's photo with Mother Teresa was placed in the entranceway of the hospital where Katherine had worked so long and hard.

One morning, her housekeeper found Dr. Katherine Kincaid in her bed. She had passed peacefully in her sleep.

Her children, grandchildren, the hospital staff, and many of her former patients attended Katherine's funeral mass which took place in St. Michael's in Calcutta. A large population gathered outside the church to say a final good-bye to the lady who had so graciously dedicated years of her life to them.

The town's people made a simple white wooden casket for Katherine and she was buried next to her husband. Over her grave they placed a plain gray tomb stone with the carving of an angel and the words: "Our Angel—Dr. K".

Katherine's dear friend, Pari, who was now a nurse, would forever tell everyone, "Dr. Katherine Kincaid was the most courageous woman I have ever met. And I know she is in Heaven with her husband and God. We were blessed to have her as our dear friend. We'll never forget her smile and her kindness."

# Articles and Short Stories

## by Raymond Weaver

"The Past Sixty Years" published in Chicken Soup for the Soul: Twins and More, March 2009-a story about Ray and his twin brother, Ed.

"A Star is Born", published in Chicken Soup for the Soul: Inspirations for the Young at Heart, August 2011-a story about Ray's appearance in a play at the local theater.

"The Cell Phone" published in Chicken Soup for the Soul: Inspirations for the Young at Heart, August 2011, a story about Ray's first experience with carrying a cell phone.

"It's A Poem" published in "Chicken Soup for the Soul-Inspiration for Writers" May 2013, a story about an elderly woman in a nursing home who inspired Ray to continue writing.

"A Grandfathers Dream", "The Wieliczka Salt Mines", "Ground Zero in New York", "So this is Canada, Eh", "Ray and Ellie visit Lourdes" among articles published in the Safety Harbor, Florida, newspaper, The Tropical Breeze.

"So this is Sterling" published in the Dunedin Florida's newspaper-The Highlander.

Make your Memories" published in the "Seniority Section" of the St. Petersburg Times.

Second place in June "Times Remembered Section" of the St. Petersburg Times with a story about his granddaughter.

Story about Grandpa Weaver's 1902 Grocery Store, published in Bend of the River magazine.

Numerous articles published in the Suncoast Hospice Newsletter.

# Author's Bio

Ray Weaver is a resident of Clearwater, Florida. He and his wife, Ellie, have been married for fifty-six years and have two children and six grandchildren. Ray has been writing for twelve years and has numerous short stories and articles published in major magazines and newspapers.

He is very proud of the four stories that he has had published in the Chicken Soup for the Soul books. "It's a Poem" was in "Chicken Soup for the Soul, Inspirations for Writers" May, 2013. "The Past Sixty Years" was in the "Chicken Soup for the Soul-Twins and More" released in March 2009. "A Star is Born" and "The Cell Phone" were featured in "Chicken Soup for the Soul-Inspirations for the Young at Heart" released in August, 2011.

His first novel, "Tightrope to Justice" was published in 2010 and his second novel, "Miami Justice" was published in August 2011". The third novel, "European Justice" was published in 2012 and the fourth, "Justice 4 Willis" was released in 2013. The fifth and final novel in the Willis family, "Final Justice" was published in 2014.

Ray loves to hear from his readers

You may contact him at raymondellie@aol.com

## Coming Next

# Three Great Men

The story of three different and great men, who made their families proud of them, sometimes risking their lives to make their dream come true.

Due out in Spring 2016

www.ingramcontent.com/pod-product-compliance
Lightning Source LLC
Chambersburg PA
CBHW072050170626
46813CB00004B/1292